LETTI'S SECOND ACT
Durango Street Theatre – Book 5

Emily Mims

ALSO BY EMILY MIMS

Durango Street Theatre
Vivi's Leading Man
Maggie's Starring Role
Wade's Dangerous Debut
Jessica's Hero

The Smoky Blues series
Mist
Smoke
Evergreen
Indigo
Emerald
Mistletoe
Violet
Ruby
Amethyst
Noelle

The Texas Hill Country series
Solomon's Choice
After the Heartbreak
A Gift of Trust
Daughter of Valor
Welcome Home
Unexpected Assets
Never and Always
A Gift of Hope
Once, Again

Other Romances
Season of Enchantment
A Dangerous Attraction
For the Thrill of It All

www.**BOROUGHSPUBLISHINGGROUP**.com

PUBLISHER'S NOTE: This is a work of fiction. Names, characters, places and incidents either are the product of the author's imagination or are used fictitiously. Any resemblance to actual events, locales, business establishments or persons, living or dead, is coincidental. Boroughs Publishing Group does not have any control over and does not assume responsibility for author or third-party websites, blogs or critiques or their content.

LETTI'S SECOND ACT
Copyright © 2020 Emily Wright Mims

ISBN 978-1-951055-85-1

To every woman who has reached for the impossible
and made her dreams come true.

ACKNOWLEDGMENTS

This book was not written in a vacuum. I would like to thank my dedicated beta readers, Edwin Floyd, Troy Bernhardt, and Sharon Middleton for their valuable input. Michelle, thank you for your perceptive editing and especially for such a gorgeous cover. She looks just like the Letti I pictured in my mind! And thanks to my copy editor, Tanya. I appreciate you all.

As with all the books in the Durango Street Theatre series, I couldn't have written this without the amazing input from the staff and volunteers of the Woodlawn Theatre. At this moment in time, the theater is closed and the marquis dark. But the incredible spirit of the wonderful people of the Woodlawn still shines bright, as they reach out to us via technology to continue to teach, entertain, and inspire. I love you all so much and look forward to the day the marquis will shine bright again, and music and song will reverberate throughout the theater once more.

LETTI'S SECOND ACT

Chapter One

Letti sat back in the uncomfortable auditorium chair and watched with a critical eye as two of her Intro to Theater students stumbled through a seven-minute vignette. There were doing a brief scene from *Oklahoma!,* the musical she'd recently finished directing at the Durango Street Theatre. Her first-year college students, mostly non-majors trying to knock out a fine arts credit, varied from the truly mediocre to downright horrible, but they had paid their tuition and deserved the same respect as her more serious students, and the talented actors she worked with at the Durango.

Her assessment of the students' performance was as kind as possible while still being honest.

"Pronunciation and enunciation weren't great, but I could understand most of your lines. Work some on the emotions in the scene. These people are truly drawn to one another. The audience needs to see that. Any questions?"

They shook their heads and practically ran off the stage. Letti checked her watch. Twenty more minutes and three more vignettes, and then she was done for the day. She was almost done for the semester, but this year she would be teaching a summer school course. She hadn't much wanted to teach a summer session, knowing most of her students would be transients in town for a couple of months with no real interest in theater. But thanks to an unanticipated car payment from an accident the previous fall, and the college expenses for her daughter, Sophie, that would begin next year, Letti needed the money more than she needed the summer off.

She would spend the time looking forward to the regular fall semester when the itinerant summer school students would go back to wherever, and she would have her regular crowd, students who cared about theater and had at least a modicum of talent. Those students were a gold mine of potential talent for the Durango, and she wasn't shy about actively recruiting the better ones to act in the quality productions at the community theater.

She sat through the remaining vignettes and doled out critiques. It was already going on three when she returned to her office long enough to stuff a stack of test papers in her briefcase to grade this evening. The hot May sunshine beat down on her as she crossed the parking lot and climbed in her crossover. She was about to pull out when her ex-husband's ringtone sounded. She looked at the screen and made a face before clicking on. "What do you need, Owen?"

"I'm stuck at the ocular prosthetics office. I'm trying to get a better-looking eye and it's taking forever. Is there any way you or Sophie can pick Marco up from practice?"

"Damn. She's at the theater and I'm heading over there."

"I hate to ask, but if I leave I don't know when I can get another appointment."

"Okay. One or the other of us will get him. Why the new eye? Your other one looks fine."

"It did until last night. Wade knocked it in the toilet and didn't realize it until after he flushed. Now I'm wearing an eyepatch and look like Captain Kidd."

She shook her head. "Whatever. Do you still want Marco for the evening?"

"Absolutely. And thanks."

She clicked off and started the engine. At least the SOB was trying these days. Devastated by facial scarring and the loss of his eye during a bomb explosion, his career as a police officer had ended. He'd holed up in his apartment for five long years, refusing to be seen and neglecting his kids in the process. She knew she should be grateful to Wade Baxter for pulling Owen out of his self-imposed isolation and persuading him to rejoin the land of the living. He was once again the father her children needed, and even up on the Durango stage again.

She pressed her lips together and fought down a wave of bitterness. What he couldn't ever be again was a husband to her. After fifteen years of marriage, he'd come to the realization that he preferred the company of men. He'd been cheating on her with a male co-star when he was injured defusing a bomb, and after almost losing his life he decided to quit trying to be someone he wasn't and came out of the closet.

Now he and his new man, Wade, were a couple.

She wasn't sure what galled her the most. The fact that Owen had ended their marriage to be with men, or that Wade was fifteen years younger than she was.

It wasn't that she disliked Wade, she loved the young man dearly and was happy he'd learned to love himself. But she envied them for having found the happiness that was still eluding her five years after her marriage had gone down the toilet.

More than once she'd chided herself for her disgruntlement over the status quo. She had two children who were the lights of her life. She lived in a nice neighborhood, and she had everything she needed and a lot of what she wanted. She made her living in the world of theater as well as spending a lot of her free time doing what she loved. From the outside looking in, she had it good. She ought to be grateful for what she had.

Never mind that she would never get to live the life she'd always dreamed of having.

Pushing that thought away, she turned the AC up to full blast and was humming a song from *Oklahoma!* by the time she got to the theater. The back door was open and she could hear the music from a couple of early Academy classes, already preparing for the summer production of *The Little Mermaid.* Both the adults and the Academy students would be doing productions of the delightful movie-turned-stage play. Mermaid tails would abound. It was going to be a lot of fun.

She detoured through the back of the theater to the wing housing the theater offices. Damn. She'd forgotten the construction crews were in the middle of installing permanent walls and doors. The largest dance studio had been temporarily commandeered to house the office staff, most of whom were at their desks. Artistic director Rachel Castillo looked up at Letti and bit her lip.

Uh-oh. Rachel always bit her lip when she had bad news to deliver.

Rachel smiled. "I wasn't expecting you until later. Crewing for the elementary production of *Oklahoma!* this weekend?"

"I am. They're too little to move the sets. The teenagers are a different story. I'll get them started and sneak up to the balcony to enjoy the show."

"It's good of you to volunteer. Especially since Marco isn't doing the Academy anymore."

Letti made a face. "He was never into it. Not like Sophie, who has lived and breathed it since she was five." She waited a beat. "You may as well spill it. Somebody's going to have to tell me whatever it is sooner or later."

Rachel's blush was visible despite her dark complexion. "Uh, Josh wanted to know if you'd be crew chief for *The Little Mermaid*."

Letti waited a beat. "I see. Crew chief. *Again.* May I ask who you cast in the female leads?"

"We cast Vivienne as Ursula. She wanted to do one more show before the baby comes. It will be too much for her to perform here when she's trying to run a company and take care of a little one."

"You're right. It will be," Letti said, choking down disappointment. She would have taken the part of Ursula in a heartbeat. "What about Ariel?"

"Josh wants to take a chance on a newbie. An Incarnate Word sophomore one of the new Academy instructors brought to auditions. You remember her. The little redhead with the big smile."

"And the iffy voice," Letti said tersely. "What in hell are you thinking? I—" She stopped and stared at Rachel.

Rachel looked Letti in the eye. "The new girl won't sing it the way you would. I get that. But Ariel's supposed to be a *girl*, Letti. Not a grown woman." *Not a forty-year-old.* Rachel sat up straighter. "You know what? I'm going to say it and if you get mad, too bad. You probably could have had the part of Ursula if you'd gotten up there and sung one of her songs. But no. You sang one of Ariel's. You may as well have come out and said you didn't want to play Ursula. You wanted to get up there and pretend you're twenty again."

Letti's face burned. "Thanks a damned lot. I would have gladly played Ursula."

"Well, hell. We didn't know that." She looked at Letti imploringly. "Please, Letti. *Think* next time you audition for a role." She paused a minute. "Are you willing to be crew chief for *Mermaid*, or should I get someone else?"

"Fine. I'll do it."

Rachel's face broke into a relieved smile. "Thanks. I appreciate it."

"Whatever."

Letti left the makeshift office, her lips tight. They could have asked her, she thought. She wouldn't have been thrilled to play the older mermaid, but she would have done it. Gladly. She didn't hate crewing. She knew it was an important contribution to the production, and a lot of fun. But backstage wasn't where she wanted to be. Where she wanted to be, where she longed to be, was on the stage, playing Dorothy in *The Wizard of Oz,* or Laurey Williams in *Oklahoma!* or maybe Maria von Trapp in *The Sound of Music.* She wanted to bring characters to life for the audiences at the Durango. As she had once dreamed of doing on the sound stages in Hollywood.

Before life intervened and that dream train derailed.

Shaking off her pique, she went in search of Sophie. One or the other of them needed to pick up Marco. She met her daughter in the lobby as Sophie came out of the Academy. "So. Have you checked with Jessica about *The Little Mermaid* casting? Has she made an official announcement yet?"

"She has. I've got Andrina."

"*Andrina?* That's totally ridiculous. That's not even a supporting part."

"There aren't but two lead parts for girls, Mom. And I can't sing alto so Ursula was out."

"Who got Ariel?"

"Emma Ellis."

"Emma Ellis?" It was one thing for them to snub her for the adult production, that she could take in stride. But they would not snub her daughter for the teen production. "What the hell is Jessica thinking? That girl can't sing her way out of a paper bag. Damn it." Letti started toward Jessica's office on the Academy side. Sophie needed that role, and Jessica knew it. Letti had no idea what the young Academy director was thinking, but Jessica had better be ready to explain herself.

Letti could hear Sophie on her heels. "Mom, *no.* Andrina's fine. I'm good with it, okay?"

She whirled around. "You are *not* good with it. Let me take care of this." She marched through the Academy and threw Jessica's office door open. She stepped in the office and shut the door in Sophie's face.

Jessica was seated in her desk chair. Letti was vaguely aware of others in the room, but all her attention was on Jessica. "What were you thinking, casting Emma Ellis as Ariel? You know as well as I do that the role should have gone to Sophie. She is by far your best soprano and she can act circles around Emma. Sophie needs that role on her résumé and you know it. And the Navarros expect quality. You really think you're going to show them quality with that child in the role?"

Jessica's eyes widened. Letti took a breath, ready to say more, when a man seated across from the desk started to clap. "Bravo. Damn, what a performance. Absolutely wonderful. You have the stage-mother-scorn routine down to a T."

Letti whirled around, prepared to give whoever he was a what-for, and sucked in her breath at the sight of Kevin Summerset staring at her with a smirk on his face. *Him.* She did a double take. No, it wasn't a look-alike. It really was Kevin. The same sun-streaked blond hair. The same dancing blue eyes. The same chiseled features and square chin. The same broad shoulders and narrow waist. The same mouth-watering appeal that had at one time been her undoing.

And now, the same sardonic smile aimed at her.

Her best dream and her worst nightmare rolled in one.

She willed her shock not to show. "Kevin Summerset. As I live and breathe. Home from Hollywood."

He raised his eyebrow. "Hello, Mrs. Aldrete. It's been awhile."

Letti swallowed. It had been awhile. Five long years since she'd gotten drunk and taken the then-twenty-year-old Kevin Summerset to a Holiday Inn a few blocks from the old Durango where they burned up the sheets. She'd just found out about Owen's affair and was looking for some payback, and Kevin had been more than willing. The alcohol and revenge-fueled night had been spectacular. Despite Kevin's inexperience, the sex had been out of this world.

Not that she'd had any desire for a repeat. The morning after had sucked. Sobered up and hung over, she had been mortified beyond belief at the depths to which she had fallen.

Kevin hadn't exactly been jailbait, but he was close. Not only that, she was still married, at least technically, and she was appalled that she had lowered herself to her cheating husband's level. She had pulled on her clothes as quickly and quietly as she could and ducked out of the motel room, leaving Kevin sleeping the sleep of the dead. Then she had cried all the way home.

To this day she got a sour taste in her mouth whenever she thought about that night.

Even though it had been, by far, and still was, the best sex of her life.

She had spent weeks on tenterhooks, dreading the moment she ran into Kevin again. Or heard about her night with him through the grapevine. She was thrilled beyond belief when she learned that he'd practically been on his way out of town, heading to Hollywood to seek his fame and fortune. She saw his parents often enough. Byron and Barbara Summerset were major supporters of the Durango, and Byron sat on the board. But Kevin must have kept their night together private since his parents never were less than the soul of graciousness anytime they had occasion to speak to Letti.

She could only hope he would continue to keep his mouth shut about their one-night stand.

Her eyes flicked from him to the pale little blonde on the other chair. Emma Ellis. Letti didn't know why he and the girl were here and she didn't much care. She turned back to Jessica.

"As Kevin said, I have the stage mother routine down pat. I will take that as high praise. At least my daughter and I can act, unlike the scared little rabbit sitting there beside Kevin. Jessica, you screwed up royally, and I'm calling you on it."

Jessica looked pissed. Letti felt a stab of guilt having said what she did in front of Emma, which she quickly stuffed down. Sophie could sing and dance rings around Emma, and they all knew it.

"I'm sorry you feel that way," Jessica said stiffly. "I for one think Emma will do a wonderful job."

"So do I," Kevin stated.

She turned to him. "An expert after five short years in Hollywood. What made you come home? Washed up in Tinseltown?"

Kevin opened his mouth, but Emma beat him to it. "No, he was doing fine in Hollywood. He had to come home. My mom was killed in a wreck and Uncle Kevin came back to help…me."

Oh, shit. In her anger, she'd forgotten that Emma's mother, a frequent ensemble player, had been killed going home last year from a rehearsal. She looked from Emma to Kevin. "I'm sorry for your loss."

Kevin didn't look at her. "Jessica, we'll talk later. You know where to find me. Mrs. Aldrete, good to see you again." He and Emma rose and exited the office.

Jessica crossed her arms in front of her and stared at Letti balefully. "Was that really necessary? You hurt that child's feelings."

"You hurt Sophie's," Letti shot back. "She needs all the good roles she can get, at least until we've sent off her college applications. Do you really think a college admissions committee's going to be impressed with the role of Andrina? And what about the scholarship committees? Think that role's going to impress them?"

"Probably not. But they will be impressed with Laurey Williams in *Oklahoma!*. And Ariel Moore in *Footloose*. And how about Audrey in *Little Shop of Horrors?* Oh, and let's not forget Reno Sweeney in *Anything Goes*. Jesus, Letti, Sophie's had plenty of leading roles. More than her share. Maybe it's time somebody else has a chance to shine."

"One more role," Letti said tightly. "One more role and then it wouldn't have mattered. The applications would have gone out. But no, it went to a child with a fraction of Sophie's talent. Why couldn't Emma have had a lead role in the upcoming winter production? After Sophie's sent everything in."

"Because she lives on a ranch south of town and the only time she can do a show is in the summer." Jessica's tone held little patience. "There are other considerations besides Sophie's resume. According to Mrs. Summerset, Emma's having a hard time coming to terms with the loss of her mother, and her alcoholic father's no help. You know it must be bad if Kevin had to come home. Have a heart, Letti. Emma needs to do this."

"So does Sophie. College costs a small fortune and Owen and I aren't rich. My girl needs some scholarship help. What are you going to tell the Navarros when *The Little Mermaid* isn't up to par? They care as much about the Academy productions as the adult." She looked Jessica in the eye. "That's your salary their contributions pay. Not mine."

Jessica sighed. "The Navarros are all about the kids, and if they say anything I will remind them of that. Letti, Sophie's got a boatload of talent. She's had plenty of leading roles to put on her résumé, and she will have more. With her talent, she will get into whatever acting school she wants and she will get it paid for one way or another. So please. Don't begrudge Emma. She doesn't have a mother fighting for her like you, or a father who cares like Owen in her corner."

"No, she has a rich grandmother coming in here telling you to cast her in the lead."

"Kind of like you do with Sophie?" Jessica smiled sweetly.

Shit. Letti stalked out of Jessica's office, trembling with fury.

She heard footsteps behind her. "Mom, wait up."

Letti kept walking. She had no desire to go another round with Sophie right now. They were almost to the lobby when her daughter caught up with her. "I can't believe you did that," Sophie hissed. "I have never been so embarrassed in all my *life*. You were so pushy, and mean."

"That's what you get for eavesdropping." Letti hid her smile. At seventeen, Sophie was every inch the drama queen. She reached out and patted Sophie's arm. "I think you'll survive it. Sweetie, I'm looking out for you. The competition to get into a top-notch acting school is fierce. You need the strongest résumé you can possibly have."

"Mom, you heard Jessica. I'll have other good roles."

"But how many before we start sending in applications? The window of opportunity is quickly closing. You'll have one more chance in the fall, and that's it."

"Mom, I have a list of credits as long as my arm," Sophie said quietly.

"So will every other kid applying for those schools. *The Little Mermaid* might have made the difference to an application committee." She looked at her beautiful daughter, her heart full of love and concern. "Honey, I lost my chance for a career in Hollywood. I don't want that to happen to you. I want you to have an opportunity to follow your dreams. If that means I have to be pushy on occasion, so be it." She glanced down at her watch. "Your brother's soccer practice will be over in fifteen minutes. Can you pick him up on the way to your father's for dinner?"

Sophie nodded and dashed away through the lobby. Letti followed more slowly. She was looking forward to having a few hours by herself to eat some takeout and grade a few tests.

She was halfway across the lobby when she noticed Kevin's familiar sun-streaked hair falling forward as he bent over to reach the under-the-counter refrigerator in the concession booth.

"Those sodas are for sale," she said dryly. "We customarily bring our own."

Kevin straightened and grinned sardonically. "I know they're for sale. I plan to sell all I can this weekend. Gotta earn my money."

What the hell? Why would he be selling sodas in the lobby?

"Did Josh hire you?"

"Sure did."

Wonderful. She'd be tripping over him all the time now, constantly reminded of the night she'd been stupid in the extreme.

"Why here? There are bound to be better jobs elsewhere. Or are you planning to be part of the theater?"

"Perfect part-time job. I can get involved with the theater, and I can be here for Emma. Which appears to be necessary given your performance in Jessica's office a few minutes ago."

"Tough. If Emma's going to do theater, she better get used to an honest assessment of her talent. Or lack of it, in her case."

"Jesus, you're hard."

"No, I'm honest. Sophie can act and sing circles around your niece. Sorry if the truth sucks." She looked him up and down, taking in the sun-bleached hair, the dark tan, the muscular body showcased by his tight tee shirt and cargo shorts. Damn if she didn't feel a tingle of attraction. "So you're back."

He nodded. "I'm back. Hollywood's not all it's cracked up to be."

"Yeah, sure." She didn't believe that for a minute.

He looked her up and down much as she had him. "Damn. You're looking good, woman." He leaned forward, a wicked grin on his lips. "Care to take up where we left off? Go for a repeat or two? That was one hell of a night."

Cheeky asshole. The hell of it was that she felt the same pull as she had five years ago. It was galling to have the hots for a man fifteen years her junior. Hell, he was closer in age to Sophie than he was to Letti. He'd been in diapers when she'd been in high school.

He wants to play? Game on. She raised an eyebrow and looked him up and down for a second time before shaking her head. "I don't think so." She reached out and patted his cheek. "The tutoring session was a fun departure, and I remember it fondly. These days I've sworn off boys and am sticking to men who know what they're doing. But thanks for the offer. See you around, hon."

She winked and sailed out before he could reply.

Her bravado lasted until she was backstage. He had no business working at *her* theater. He should have stayed in Hollywood where she wouldn't have to think about him and remember the night she'd made a total fool of herself. She wouldn't have to remember how appealing the he looked wearing nothing but a come-hither smile. How he'd felt taking her over and over, his youthful lust and enthusiasm more than making up for his inexperience when he was bringing her to climax more times than she could count.

If he'd stayed where he belonged, she wouldn't have to admit she found him as appealing as ever.

Chapter Two

Tutoring session?

Damn. Had he been that bad in bed?

Kevin watched as Letti sauntered across the lobby and through the swinging doors into the auditorium. He didn't know whether he should take her jab seriously. He had been awfully young and inexperienced that night. But if memory served, she'd enjoyed a number of orgasms, and he had learned a thing or two under her tutelage. Knowledge that had served him well in LA.

But he'd never had the same unrelenting drive to keep fucking a woman as he'd had for Letti Aldrete in that downtown Holiday Inn.

As he adjusted his shorts, he acknowledged she still did it for him.

He laughed at himself and unloaded the rest of the sodas into the refrigerator. Why he had such an insane desire for the woman he didn't know. Sure, she was absolutely, positively gorgeous, with a classic face, and high, perfectly molded cheekbones. Her lips were lush and kissable and she had a banging body. All curves and secrets.

But cougars were not his thing.

He pried open a case of beer and started sliding the cans into the fridge.

Maybe it was her eyes. Somewhere between brown and amber, they were mesmerizing, especially sparking with anger and sass—or better yet, brimming with passion.

More than once he'd dreamed of that night, waking up as hard as a rock. He'd tried in vain to find that special something with other women, and had enjoyed a number of delightful ladies in the process. But he'd never quite recreated that night, and had given up trying.

Now he was home and working at the theater where she and her daughter spent a lot of time. If Letti's reaction was to be believed, she wasn't interested in an encore performance.

He wasn't sure he believed she wasn't interested. The heat in her eyes when she was top-to-toeing him told quite a different story.

Maybe, if he played his cards right, she would be up for a little something-something.

After he finished loading the beer, he cut open a case of bottled water.

Perhaps he should find out if she's still married or otherwise attached before he made any moves. He remembered she and her husband had been acting with another husband-wife team in that year's production of *White Christmas*. Kevin had been part of the ensemble, and had learned a lot watching the four lead actors, who, while "amateurs," were incredibly talented performers.

As he thought back to the show's run, he recalled the first half had gone smoothly, but there had been considerable tension during the second half, with tightly whispered conversations and *fuck off* looks between Letti and her husband.

At the cast party celebrating the end of the run, Letti had looked Kevin in the eye and asked if he wanted to fuck her. Well, she'd said it more euphemistically, but that was the gist.

He couldn't say he knew much about her outside their night in a hotel room.

As of today, he knew she was Sophie's mother, and she didn't take kindly to other girls getting roles she wanted for her daughter. He again thought of her throwdown in Jessica's office and his lips tipped up in a smile.

Even though she had been rude to Emma, Letti had been magnificent. All fire and passion.

That he remembered well.

He finished loading the water and laid out the candy bars and popcorn bags. When he was satisfied the concession stand was ready, he ducked back into the Academy, passing through the studios, and stuck his head in Jessica's office, where she and a plump woman with curly graying hair he recognized as production manager Miranda Jenks were staring at the computer screen.

"It's me again."

Jessica swung around and looked at him ruefully. "I thought you might be back after Letti's set-to. Is Emma okay?"

"I hope so. She scurried off for class the minute we walked out of here. Tell me, is Sophie that much better? Is she going to make trouble for Emma?"

The women looked at one another. "To be honest, Sophie is the most talented young person to come through the Academy in all the years I've worked here," Miranda said slowly. "One of the best I've ever seen."

"I would have to second that," Jessica added. "She has the talent to make it in New York, Hollywood, or anyplace she wants to work."

Kevin felt his face fall. "So she's going to be trouble for Emma."

"No. Absolutely not. She's not going to be one bit of trouble," Jessica said firmly.

"Sophie's one of the sweetest, kindest girls we have in the program," Miranda added. "She is the last one who would be unkind or spiteful."

"Letti will be all right, too. Once she gets down off her high horse. She'll be a little snarky, but otherwise okay," Jessica said.

"Then what was today all about?" Kevin asked.

Jessica said, "She was already ticked because she didn't get a role in the adult production. Rachel was going to ask her to take crew chief again. My casting Emma punched her last button."

"Letti does it to herself," Miranda said dryly. "If she would take age-appropriate roles, she could act all she wants. Did she audition one of Ariel's songs?"

Jessica sighed. "You nailed it."

"Interesting," Kevin said slowly. "Why is she so determined to play ingénue roles? More importantly, why is she so pushy about Sophie, especially if the girl's as talented as you say she is?"

"Well," Miranda said, drawing out the word as she shut the door. "What I'm about to say isn't a secret. Trust me, everyone here knows this story in detail."

"Okay," he said when it seemed like she wasn't going to continue.

"Letti's probably one of the most talented performers our adult troupe ever had. I've been with the Durango a long time, and considering some of the talent that graced our stage, that's saying a lot."

"Truly, she would have made it," Jessica said. "She'd bucked her family's expectations and had gone to USC as an acting major. That's where she met Owen, and got to know him a little too well, if you get what I mean."

"She got pregnant," he surmised.

"Yes, in the middle of their senior year," Jessica continued. "She and Owen are decent people. I don't know if they would've stayed together if she hadn't gotten pregnant, but they did the old-fashioned thing, got married, and came back here. Letti had Sophie, and her dad helped Owen get a spot in the police academy. Letti returned to school and received her MFA from Texas State. She's been teaching at the community college for years. She and Owen had a second child, Marco, and she went on with her life, but she's never made it a secret how disappointed she is about missing out on her chance at fame and fortune."

"Jesus. How does that make her kids feel?" Kevin asked. "Especially the girl. She has to know she's the reason her mother gave up her dreams."

Miranda laughed. "I doubt it bothers Sophie, and Marco is oblivious. Letti has made it her mission in life to make damned sure Sophie will have the chance Letti didn't. By the time Sophie was five or six, it was obvious she inherited her parents' talent. Letti's been grooming her ever since."

"No wonder she was upset about Emma being cast as Ariel," Kevin said.

Jessica sighed. "It gets old. Her mission has become an obsession. Today was the nastiest she's ever been, but she and I have had these discussions before."

"And her insistence on the ingénue roles?" he asked.

Miranda rolled her eyes. "That started after the divorce. She and Owen had a contentious, public parting of the ways a few years back. It started during *White Christmas* and she's been bitter ever since."

White Christmas. That was when they'd had their night together. "What happened during *White Christmas?*" he asked, trying to sound casual.

"She found out Owen was cheating on her." Miranda shook her head at the memory.

Huh. Five years later, and now he finds out he was a revenge fuck. He'd wondered more than once what her motivation had been for picking him up that night. Now he wished he hadn't found out. "Who was he cheating with? Was it somebody in the cast?" That would explain the glares and the whispers.

Miranda sighed. "Letti thought it was her co-star Beth Roberts, but it turned out to be Beth's husband, Johnny. After Owen almost died in an explosion, he came out 'officially.' Recently, he took up with Wade Baxter."

Kevin thought a minute. "I think I met them the other night. They're playing Will Parker and Jud Fry, right?"

Jessica nodded. "I didn't know her then, but she's still a little bitter about the divorce."

"After all she gave up to find out Owen was cheating on her right under her nose, I'd be bitter too," Miranda said.

"Explains her desire to turn back the clock," Kevin mused.

"It's a shame she feels that way," Jessica said. "With her looks and her talent, she could be rocking the stage. There are plenty of parts for forty-year-olds."

"Anyway, enough about Letti and her drama." Miranda turned the conversation. "Tell us about you. You did a couple of shows with us and then you left for LA, and now you're back. Is this an extended visit, or are you home to stay?"

"I'm home to stay." It felt surprisingly good to say that out loud. "Emma's not in good shape after losing Renee, and Mom and Dad are still knocked for a loop even though they don't let on in public."

Jessica's face softened. "I'm sorry that's why you had to come home. We miss your sister."

"Thank you. We miss her too. Emma misses her the most. My parents and I will be eternally grateful to you for casting her as Ariel. It'll give her something to focus on beside her mother and her deadbeat father."

Jessica and Miranda both winced.

"Are you gonna miss LA?" Miranda asked. "The sound stages? The beaches? The starlets? The glamour?"

"The sucky agents? The traffic? The cattle calls? The few and far between walk-on parts? Waiting tables to feed my face? No, I won't miss it. Five years was quite enough, thank you very much. Maybe I shouldn't admit this, but I was thinking about coming home anyway. Losing Renee only sped up the timetable."

"What's next then?" Jessica asked.

"I'm starting law school in the fall. St. Mary's. I figure the courtroom's as good a place as a sound stage to put my theatrical talent to good use."

"You're probably right," Jessica laughed. "But after five years, I bet you racked up some really good stories."

He had, and he spent the next few minutes sharing a couple. Then it was time to make the long drive to Emma's home on the Red Rock Ranch in Atascosa County.

After she got in his car, he tried several times to draw her into conversation, but after a couple of one-word replies he gave up and drove on in silence.

He hoped Emma didn't take Letti's unkind words to heart. She didn't appear to. Maybe she was already acquainted with Letti's snark. Or maybe the temper tantrum was minor, especially compared with losing her mother, and the verbal abuse her father was capable of inflicting when he was sloshed. Kevin wished his mother and father would sue for custody. Emma would be so much better off with them.

Even when Emma's mother, Renee, was alive, she wasn't like Letti, who might be a pain in the ass, but it was clear she loved her daughter and would do anything for her. Even change the course of her life. Letti would never know whether she could have made it in the industry.

Unlike him. He'd had his chance. He'd gone to LA. He'd had his shot at and learned it wasn't all it was cracked up to be. He was glad to be home.

Knowing what he did, and that whatever he experienced, it was worse for women, made him wonder if Letti would have liked it as much as she thought she would. Perhaps. She had the determination and passion necessary to persevere.

The very qualities that made her more attractive than five years ago when she'd rocked his world in a motel room and ruined him for every woman who followed her. After hearing her backstory, he admired her. Her devotion to her daughter. Her willingness to give up her dreams to make a family. Her determination to see her child achieve what she had not.

He smirked.

He'd love another tutoring session from her.

Chapter Three

Letti stood at the foot of the steps, looked up in frustration and yelled, "Sophie. Marco. Time to get a move on. Both of you."

"I can't, Mom," Marco hollered down the steps. "Sophie's got the bathroom tied up."

"Sophie, *hurry*. Your dad's picking Marco up in ten minutes."

Letti heard the toilet flush, and shook her head, wondering what was taking her daughter so long. Sophie was usually in and out of the bathroom rather quickly.

She returned to the kitchen and popped a pod in the coffeemaker then started unloading the dishwasher while the coffee brewed. It was shaping up to be a busy weekend.

Sophie would be at the theater all day today, and then she had a cookout organized by one of the other Academy parents. Tomorrow after Mass, Sophie and her engineering club friends were working on yet another entry into one of the endless contests their club sponsor found for them.

Marco would be with Owen and Wade, but Letti would attend Marco's soccer game this afternoon. She had a boatload of papers to pore through, and a couple of final exams to write. And sitting in her e-reader was the latest Jonathan Kellerman mystery downloaded and ready to go for a much-needed quiet Saturday night.

Her mother had tried to fix her up on yet another blind date, but Letti had quashed that. "Not this weekend. I need some time by myself," she'd said firmly, ignoring her mother's exasperation.

Letti looked at the wall clock again. Damn it, they were all going to be late. She returned to the stairwell, only to meet Marco coming down. His hair was damp and he was dressed in his soccer practice clothes, carrying a large duffel.

"Do you have your uniform and your clothes for tomorrow?"

"Yes, all packed and ready to go." His voice cracked on the last word and dropped an octave. He blushed with embarrassment. "Sorry about that."

"Don't be. You're probably going to have your father's voice."

"Ya think?" This time his voice went treble on the last word.

"I know."

"That would be cool."

"It would." Owen's deep, velvety, almost mesmerizing voice was one of his greatest assets in the theater. "Now, get in the kitchen and kill that bowl of cereal before your father gets here. You don't want to be late for practice."

Her gangly son ducked into the kitchen, and Letti stared after him. Marco was looking more like Owen every day. The same square jaw, high cheekbones and warm brown eyes. The same jaunty smile. He was going to be taller than his father, but otherwise their builds were similar.

Thank God Owen had come to his senses and stepped back up as a dad. More than once she'd wondered if Marco was gay too. He was so shy and often couldn't look her in the eye, like he had a secret. She'd said something to Wade who laughed a little and told her, "I promise you, the way that boy turns red and stammers any time there's a pretty girl around, he's not gay. Right now, he's in the painfully shy stage. It'll pass."

Marco was pouring his cereal when the doorbell rang. Damn. Owen was early. She opened the door and made herself smile at her former husband, this morning sporting an eyepatch. It made him look like a pirate.

"I take it you're still waiting on your new eyeball. Come on in. I'll tell Marco to get a move on."

"No, don't do that," he said quickly. He stepped in and pulled the door shut after him. "I came early because I want to talk to you for a moment." Owen looked hesitant and Letti felt a red flag go up.

She gestured toward the seldom-used living room. He sat down on the sofa and motioned for her to do the same. Instead she sat across from him in an armchair. From this angle, she could see both the damaged and undamaged sides of his face. What happened to him was so unfair.

He'd been trying to defuse a bomb when his reckless partner had jumped in and cut the wrong wire. The partner died and Owen had been left with only one eye and facial scarring from hell. The PD medically retired him, and he was still trying to build up his web page design business. Thanks to Wade, Owen wasn't hiding away any longer, and was again involved at the Durango. She looked at him with alarm. "Don't tell me you and Wade broke up. I hope that's not what you want to talk to me about."

Owen shook his head, his expression serious. "Quite the opposite. I popped the question last night. Wade said yes. We're getting married."

Married. Letti stared at Owen. "I gather you're not going to ask Father Hinojosa to perform the ceremony."

Owen cracked a smile. "Hardly. We'll have a judge do the honors. Maybe ask Wade's uncle up in Verde to perform the ceremony. But we intend to make it a celebration." He looked at her hesitantly. "I wanted you to hear it from me."

Letti bit back the snark that wanted to come out of her mouth. "Thank you for that." She swallowed and took a deep breath. "And congratulations. Wade's the best thing that ever happened to you. I'm happy for both of you."

"I owe you."

"What for?"

"The butt-chewing you gave me about Wade. I got in the car the next morning and put things back together with him."

"You're welcome. If you need any more butt-chewing sessions, tell Wade to let me know."

He laughed, then sobered. "Thanks, Letti. It means a lot."

He got up and held out his hand to her, pulling her to her feet and kissing her gently on the cheek. She breathed in the fresh aftershave he'd used ever since she'd known him, and fought back a wave of sorrow. She had been so in love with him at one time. While that kind of love had died awhile back, she still cared for the father of her children, and no doubt always would. "Thanks for telling me. Are you going to tell the kids?"

"I'll talk to Marco today and Sophie the next time I see her."

"Good. They'll be happy for you."

Owen nodded. He collected Marco and was out the door. She stared out the front window as they drove away, blinking back tears as he turned the corner. Damn, it hurt. Which was ridiculous. They'd been divorced for years. There had never been any possibility of a reconciliation. What she'd told Owen was true. Wade *was* the best thing that had ever happened to him.

It shouldn't hurt this much. It shouldn't hurt at all.

Maybe it wasn't hurt she was feeling. Maybe it was envy. And a little self-pity.

Owen had put his life back together. He'd found his happy ever after. He'd found the person who was going to love him for the rest of his life. Five long years and she was still floundering, alone and not sure she even wanted to find "the next one." She wasn't sure what would make her happy and put the same kind of smile on her face that was on Owen's.

Forever hovering at the edges was dreaming of a life that would never, ever happen for her.

Sighing, she turned away from the window. Damn it, where was her daughter? "Sophie," she bellowed. "You have five minutes to get down here, or you leave in whatever state you find yourself."

Sophie trudged down the stairs five minutes later, dressed in her usual rehearsal clothes. She carried a duffel, which probably held clothes for the cookout. "I'll make toast to take with me."

Letti started to object but caught herself. Toast in the car was all Sophie had time for at this point. "What took you so long?"

"I was on Skype with one of the other engineering club members. We're trying to come up with a preliminary design to take to the meeting tomorrow."

"And that's worth being late to rehearsal this morning?"

Sophie's lips tightened. "It's important to me. Mr. Ortega thinks the club has a shot at a state championship this year."

"That's all well and good. But the engineering club's not getting you into a major acting college. The Academy is. Now pack up your toast and get gone."

Sophie stuffed the toast in a paper bag and took off in the old car Owen had given her.

Letti threw a load of towels in the dryer and wandered out to her car for a trip across town where her mother and grandmother would be waiting for the *pan dulce* and *conchas* she'd bring, along with egg and chorizo breakfast tacos.

She made a quick stop at the bakery and the taco truck parked alongside it and five minutes later pulled into the driveway of the house her mother and grandmother shared.

While the neighborhood of small bungalows wasn't derelict, the houses were a far cry from the two-story well-maintained homes in her subdivision north of the inner loop.

More than once Letti had pressed her mother to sell her house and buy something nicer. With her widow's pension from SAPD and her job at an insurance agency, plus the money her frugal parents had saved, her mother could easily afford it.

But Carmela Lopez was not interested in moving, protesting that the neighborhood was safe and that the neighbors looked out for one another.

Letti knocked and her mother threw open the door a moment later. "*Hola, mija.* Come in. Your *abuelita*'s been looking forward to the *pan dulce* all week."

Letti stepped in and pulled the door shut behind her. She could smell her grandmother's favorite cinnamon-flavored coffee and hear her doing something out in the kitchen. "If the coffee's ready, we can eat. We don't want to let the tacos get cold," Letti said.

She followed her mother through the small living room and past the dining room and home altar that her grandmother insisted they have.

Concepcion Cruz had grown up deep in the heart of Mexico and was about to go into a convent when she met and married Letti's grandfather, but her *abuela* never gave up the deeply ingrained religious values of her youth. Nor had she given up her traditional ideas of how a proper Mexican girl was to behave. Which had led to many fights over the years, especially when Letti insisted on going her own way, uninterested in living the old-fashioned life her grandmother expected of all the women in the family.

Sometimes Letti felt sorry for her mother, caught in the middle and fighting a hopeless battle to reconcile her mother's ancient expectations with her daughter's modern outlook.

The aroma of coffee filled the bright, cheerful kitchen. *Abuela* leaned against her walker and fumbled with the cutlery for three. "Hola, *Abuelita*." Letti kissed her grandmother's cheek. "Want me to get that for you?"

"No, *mija. Pero dame* some coffee, *por favor.*" *Abuela* often talked in the English and Spanish combo spoken by many San Antonians.

Letti poured them all coffee while Mom set plates around the table. They sat and crossed themselves for a brief prayer. *Abuela*'s eyes lit up when Letti unwrapped the *pan dulce* and put two of the huge rolls on her plate. "That looks *delicioso. Gracias.*"

Mom took only one in deference to her diabetes. "Not that this flour tortilla's much better for me," she laughed as she opened one of the foil-wrapped tacos. She turned to Letti. "Have you been watching your sugar? You're getting to the age where problems start to kick in."

Letti nodded, tamping down the spurt of irritation. She didn't appreciate the reminder she had piled up that many birthdays. "That and the blood pressure and the cholesterol and all those other things that are supposed to be plaguing me and aren't."

"Just checking," her mother said mildly. She dumped a spoonful of salsa into the taco. "Raimundo Dias was diagnosed with diabetes last week. He's only forty-two."

"He's also over three hundred pounds and never met a pineapple upside down cake he didn't love," Letti said. "Please don't compare me to him."

They were quiet for a few minutes while Letti's grandmother polished off the second roll and wiped her mouth. "*Cómo están* Sophia and Marco? They haven't come to see us *en mucho tiempo.*"

"They were here last weekend," Letti reminded her grandmother. "I'll make a point of getting them over here soon."

"They should be over here to see us every weekend," *Abuela* said firmly. "You have never made *la familia importante* the way you should."

"I get them over here as often as I can," Letti replied equally firmly. "Sophie's theater and that engineering club she loves so much take up a lot of time, as do Marco's sports. If Sophie's going to get into USC or another acting college, she needs a quality résumé, and to have one she has to spend a lot of time at the theater. We've had this discussion before, *Abuelita.*"

"And will have it again," her mother said tiredly. "Mama, things are different now than they were when you raised me. We see more of Sophie than most grandmothers would. And Letti takes us to mass nearly every Sunday."

Abuela sniffed. "And what about Marco? What's he doing this weekend?"

Letti stifled a grin. Her grandmother wasn't going to like this. "He's with Owen and Wade. It's his dad's weekend with him."

"Does he have to spend so much time with *el pervertido*?" her grandmother snapped. "And the *querido*? You let him be around him too?"

"Yes, he has to spend time with his father," Letti said, not bothering to hide her irritation. "They both do. I couldn't stop Owen from seeing them even if I wanted to. Which I don't. Owen's the only father Marco has. The man has finally come out of his funk and is acting like a dad again, and I'm damned glad he is. Marco needs a dad. Wade is one of the nicest people I've ever known, and I am more than fine with Marco spending time with them. I'm even fine with them getting married, which is coming up soon. Owen proposed last night and Wade accepted."

Her grandmother sucked in her breath and crossed herself. "*Dios mio*. What is the world coming to? That's wrong. *Es un pecado*. A sin. What if Marco wants to be like them?"

Letti barely refrained from rolling her eyes. "For crying out loud, *Abuelita*, homosexuality's not catching."

"That's not what Father Hinojosa says."

"Really? We're taking Father Hinojosa's word for it? When did he become an expert on human sexuality?" She raised her eyebrow and nailed her grandmother with a pointed look.

"Letti, we're worried. That's all," Mom said gently.

"Don't be. Please. I'm more worried about some girl getting her claws in him, as good-looking as he's getting to be." She reached in the bag and fished out a roll.

"How are things going at the theater?"

Letti jumped on the change of subject and regaled them with the news that another girl had been cast as Ariel. "I gave Jessica a piece of my mind, not that it did any good. But I was already ticked at having to crew chief again and that was the last straw."

"You could always turn them down," her mother reminded her. "They could get someone else to head up the crew."

"I could. But I'd rather work as crew chief than have no part in the production at all." She sipped her cooling coffee.

"You spend too much time at the theater. You need to be dating again," *Abuela* said.

Letti turned to her grandmother in mock surprise. "You want me to go out with *men*? And here I thought you believed unmarried Mexican women should be locked up in a tower." Her grandmother gave her a withering glare.

"For once I agree with your grandmother," Mom said. "I don't have a thing against the theater. Your friends down there are nice. But face it, Letti, there aren't all that many men down there who are anywhere near your age, and too many of the ones who are close to your age are like Owen."

"Mom," Letti protested.

"All right. When's the last time a man at the Durango showed any interest in you whatsoever?"

Day before yesterday? Unbidden, the thought of Kevin's frank appraisal and invitation for a repeat came to mind and she blushed furiously. "Not that long ago, if you must know."

"Has anything come of it? *Will* anything come of it?"

Letti gritted her teeth. "No. It won't."

"My point exactly. You need to broaden your base, so to speak. Get to know other people. Sonia Rodriguez suggested that you might enjoy meeting—"

"*No.* I am not going out on another blind date with some loser."

Her grandmother glared. "Don't talk to your mother that way."

Letti turned to her mother. "I'm sorry, but I have no interest in being fixed up with any more of your friends' brothers, uncles, or good buddies from high school. My time is precious and I don't want to waste it on pointless blind dates."

"If you don't put yourself out there, how are you ever going to meet anyone?" Mom asked patiently.

"Who says I have to meet anyone? There's nothing wrong with the life I have now."

Which is why you were feeling sorry for yourself earlier this morning.

She was lying through her teeth and she knew it. So did they.

"If there was nothing wrong with the life you have now, you'd be a lot happier," her grandmother said. "You haven't been happy since that *bastardo* left you."

"Letti, even if you're good with it now, do you really want to spend the rest of your life alone?" Mom pressed. "Sonia wants you to meet her younger brother Diego. He's somewhere in his forties and owns a string of upscale hair salons in San Antonio and Austin. She says he's urbane and sophisticated."

"Hmm. An urbane and sophisticated hairdresser." Letti shook her head. "Mom, I've had one gay man. I don't need another."

"Sonia swears he's not gay. If anything, he's too much a ladies' man." *Great, another cheater.* "Please, Letti. Give him a chance. You never know. You might hit it off wonderfully."

"And I might waste an evening I'd rather be doing something else." She thought a minute. "Tell you what. I'll go out with him after one of the shows. That way I don't waste an entire evening. I'm crewing all the children's *Oklahoma!* productions. He can pick me up at the theater after I'm done with one of those."

"He's not going to want to go out that late," her grandmother argued. "You're making it *dificil*."

"Exactly," Letti said. "If he's all that interested, he'll go out after the show. It'll be a good way to see how interested he really is."

"Whatever, *mija*." Mom sounded resigned. "I'll give Sonia your contact information. Sonia swears he's good looking."

"*Muy guapo*," *Abuela* echoed.

That was the closest her grandmother would ever come to saying a man had sex appeal.

Okay, Letti would give Diego Rodriguez a chance. She would let her mother arrange the date. She would see for herself if the man was all his sister claimed. If he was appealing in the least.

She would see how he stacked up in appeal compared to the infuriatingly sexy Kevin Summerset.

Chapter Four

Kevin yawned and rubbed his hand down the stubble on his cheeks. The coffee in the insulated mug in his Mustang's cupholder was only doing so much this morning. He'd made the mistake of staying out late with a group of friends from high school and had gotten only a few hours of sleep before starting the long drive toward his brother-in-law's ranch south of Jourdanton, deep in Atascosa County. Over an hour's drive each way, he would be making the trip twice today or a second one tomorrow, depending on whether Emma spent the night with her grandparents. He hoped she opted to stay the night with them and go home tomorrow. The more time she spent away from her asshole father, the better off she would be.

The top was down and warm May air whipped his hair in every direction. Kevin breathed in the aroma of grass and wildflowers, and the pungent stink of cow patties. For the most part, the bluebonnets were gone, but bright yellow flowers—he wasn't quite sure what they were— blanketed the roadsides and crept into the pastureland.

Cows with their newborn calves beside them munched on lush grass. In other fields, corn and wheat plants were coming along, and more than one field was planted with the strawberries the county was famous for. Farmhouses dotted the landscape, modest homes built from the profits of cattle and crops, and big ones most likely built with oil money.

Kevin mentally tipped his hat as he drove by a pumping well. The money from a couple of oil wells on his great-grandfather's farm in the nineteen twenties had made it possible for his grandfather and his father to get their law degrees and set up highly successful law practices. Even though the oil money had long dried up, to this day, the family was enjoying the benefits from that infusion of wealth.

He passed through the sleepy town of Jourdanton and drove another fifteen miles before turning onto a rutted drive and passing across the cattle guard into the Red Rock Ranch. Which was a ludicrous name, as Kevin had yet to see a red rock anywhere on the premises.

The ranch, which was split almost evenly between cattle pastures and plowed fields, was a sandy loam that, given proper care, would have been incredibly fertile. But the ranch had suffered for years under poor management as first Cornelius Ellis, and later his son Ross, overgrazed and overplanted. Consequently, yields were a fraction of what they once had been. The ranch had limped along for years, and if his father could be believed, it was in danger of going under. Which would be heartbreaking for his niece, Emma. That ranch was her birthright, whether she chose to sell it someday or keep it going.

He hoped her whiskey-soaked father didn't lose it all.

He bounced along the rutted drive for another half mile and pulled up in front of the large but rundown ranch house. Built in better times, the place had taken on a forlorn air long before his sister's death, and only gotten worse since her passing, with peeling paint and neglected flowerbeds, and a front porch that was beginning to sag in spots.

He ran up the steps and knocked on the front door hoping Emma and not Ross would answer. But luck was not with him. His bleary-eyed brother-in-law pulled open the door, wincing as the light hit his eyes. The once-handsome man looked older than his years, grief and alcohol putting deep grooves around his mouth and eyes. His clothes hung loosely on his frame, and his expression was grim as he surveyed Kevin.

"What the hell are you doing here? I told Emma to call you and tell you she's not coming."

Kevin looked at Ross with disdain. "I never got any such message. And if I had, I would have ignored it. Where's Emma? Time's wasting."

"I'm right here, Uncle Kevin." Emma came down the stairs carrying a duffel bag. "Daddy, I told you I have to be there. I can do whatever it is you want me to do tomorrow." She lifted her chin. "I made a commitment and I intend to keep it."

"Tough shit. You're my kid and you'll stay home if I tell you to. For that matter, I have a good mind to pull you out of that stupid mess altogether. That damned theater's nothing but trouble. I don't know why you want to be part of it, anyway. It cost your mother her life."

Emma sucked in her breath and looked at Ross in dismay.

Kevin glared at Ross, not bothering to hide his contempt. "No, the drunk driver who came out of nowhere and hit Renee's car cost my sister her life. You know, this might not be the time to pull that 'you're my kid and you'll stay home if I tell you to' shit. You sure as hell don't want to pull her out of the program altogether."

"Why the fuck not?" Ross demanded.

Kevin took a step forward, deliberately crowding into Ross's space. The men were of equal height, but Kevin was broader and considerably younger. And, at the moment, angrier.

"Because you've got a pair of rich, pissed-off in-laws who know every judge in three counties and who would *love* an excuse to take your sorry ass to court and get custody of Emma. You've got a brother-in-law who's ready to testify that you stink like cheap whiskey at nine in the morning. And you've got a daughter who turns eighteen in four short months, who, at that point, will be able to decide for herself where she wants to live. At the rate you're going it probably won't be with you. *Comprende?*"

Ross curled his lip. "God-damn rich-assed Summersets. Gotta throw your weight around. Gotta have your fucking way all the time. Gotta get Emma involved at that theater whether it's good for her or not, just like her mother. Gotta come between a man and his only child."

"Daddy, it's not Pops and Babs coming between us. It's your drinking," Emma said quietly. She stepped around her father and slipped out the door.

Ross stared after his daughter, his expression unfathomable.

"Out of the mouths of babes," Kevin murmured. He looked his brother-in-law in the eye. "Damn it, man. When are you gonna pull your shit together?" He looked out at Emma, getting into the car. "You keep it up, you *will* lose her. Or she'll have to bury you. One of the two." He turned on his heel and stomped down the stairs, leaving Ross on the porch.

Emma had stowed the duffel in the back seat and was waiting on the passenger side. Kevin slid in beside her and turned on the engine. "Well, that was fun."

"He's been drunk most of the week," Emma said quietly.

"Any idea what set him off?"

Emma looked at him in surprise. "You don't remember? Mom would have turned forty on Wednesday."

Kevin winced. "No, I didn't. I'm terrible with birthdays. You think that's what did it?"

"I'm pretty sure. I heard him crying in his room for a couple of nights."

"Well, hell." Damn. The last thing he wanted to feel for Ross Ellis was pity. "Still no excuse to be drunk all week."

"No, it isn't. And it's not right to blame all the drinking on Mom dying. He drank plenty when she was alive." Emma was silent for a minute. "Do you think I would be terrible if I did move out? I could live with Pops and Babs and finish high school in San Antonio."

"No, you wouldn't be terrible at all. It might be the wake-up call your father needs to get his act together. But it's a big step and you need to think long and hard about it."

"I'll think about it. I promise."

The ride into town was mostly quiet. The shit with Ross sucked. For all his faults, he'd been good to Renee, and she'd loved him. But the stress of the deteriorating ranch and a weakness for alcohol had started him down the rabbit hole, and losing Renee had shoved him even further along. Kevin hoped Ross straightened up before he lost his daughter as well.

The theater parking lot was full. Emma disappeared into the Academy wing and he spent the morning cleaning the lobby and restrooms and setting up the concession stand for tonight's performance before going home for a much-needed nap. His mother picked Emma up from the theater and had an early supper on the table. Dinner table conversation centered around Emma's day at rehearsals.

His niece's eyes sparkled as she told them about her day. "Jessica's wonderful," she gushed. "She can listen and immediately knows what I need to do to make it sound better. Sophie's almost as good. She helped me a lot too."

"I-isn't that th-the girl who w-wanted the p-part?" Barbara Summerset asked.

Kevin had told them of the altercation with Letti, and his mother was worried, which intensified her stutter.

"Yes. But she's been super nice. It might have been mostly her mother who wanted it for her," Emma said. *Ya think?* "Anyway, Sophie was wonderful."

Kevin polished off his meal and kissed his mother's cheek. "Thanks for dinner. You don't know how many nights I would have given anything for a plate of your chicken."

"Th-thanks." His mother smiled at him. "I-it's good to h-have you h-home."

"It's good to be home. Gotta go earn money."

The Saturday evening traffic was a little heavy, but he made it to the theater with time to spare. The lobby was deserted. He started down the list Josh had given him, printed up and organized the will-call tickets, and put change in the money drawer. He was starting the popcorn machine as the cast and their parents started drifting in.

The elementary cast performed tonight, which meant the theater would be packed, mostly with proud families showing up in groups, as well as a considerable number of the Durango's adult performers here to see their young protégés at work.

He stepped into the concession stand and was dishing up the first batch of popcorn when he spotted Letti coming through the front door. This was the first time he'd seen her since their run-in a week and a half ago. The first time he'd seen her in person, at least. He'd dreamed about her a couple of times, waking up hard as a rock, and she'd been featured in a couple of fantasies of his in the shower.

She spotted him behind the counter and made a beeline to the counter. "Thank goodness you're up and running." She shoved a couple of bills at him. "Sparkling water if you have it. Regular water if you don't. I'm parched."

He fished a Topo Chico out of the refrigerator and handed her the bubbly water with a flirty smile. "Looking good, woman." She wore the inevitable black of a crew member. But the slacks were dressy and molded her awesome ass and legs to perfection. The V-neck sweater, dotted with sparkly sequins, clung lovingly to her abundant breasts, and dipped low enough to show more than a hint of cleavage.

She'd gone to some trouble with her makeup, with deeply red lips and smoky gray eyeshadow emphasizing the depths of her eyes. He leaned in closer and lowered his voice. "If I didn't know better, I'd think you were trying to seduce somebody tonight."

Her eyes danced and her smile was sultry. "Maybe I am. I have a date after the show."

A date? He reared back and looked at her, unable to ignore the jab of jealousy. "You do?"

"Believe me, I don't dress like this for the eight-year-olds."

"Uh, well, have a good time," he stammered.

"I intend to. Thanks for the Topo." She picked up the water and he watched as she sashayed through the lobby.

Damn, that sucked. Despite the way she'd shot him down with the tutoring crack, he'd been hoping he'd be able to get her to go out with him, and then make sure one thing led to another.

He should've asked Jessica and Miranda about Letti's love life.

The concession stand did brisk business until showtime. He restocked the candy and straightened up the bathrooms. The first act had a few minutes left before intermission. He slipped into the theater and stood beside Jessica, who was perched on a stool next to the sound engineer. Kevin was blown away by the skilled dancing during the ballet sequence. He'd heard the young dancers were Academy students who also danced for the local ballet company.

He watched until almost the end of the act before ducking out and taking his place behind the concession counter. Business was even more brisk during intermission and he breathed a sigh of relief when the house lights dimmed. It took the better part of the second act for him to clean up the cups, popcorn sacks and soda cans from the lobby, and to make one final pass through the restrooms.

He was shutting down the concession stand when the young cast made their way to the lobby to shake hands and greet their admiring audience.

The girls were clutching bouquets, and the boys were smiling proudly and accepting their deserved accolades. The families were in no hurry to go, so it was a good half-hour before the crowd in the lobby began to thin.

As the last of the families drifted out, the door opened and a middle-aged man slipped in, looking a bit put out. He wasn't all that tall, but he was good-looking, with high cheekbones and a Roman nose. Kevin recognized the sport shirt and dress pants as designer, and the watch as costing at least four figures.

Even the dude's haircut screamed sophistication and money. Probably a relative of one of the performers, Kevin thought as the man got out his phone and typed in a text.

Or maybe not, he thought a minute later, when Letti came from the auditorium into the lobby. She looked around a moment, finally spotting the man standing close to the door. He looked up and saw her at about the same time. Her smile was brilliant as she crossed the lobby to greet him. He clasped her hand in his, and together they walked out the door into the balmy evening.

Well, hell. That SOB wouldn't need any tutoring. He'd know exactly how to please a woman in bed.

Kevin clenched his fist. He wanted to punch something. If that was the kind of man Letti favored, no way would she want to go back to bed with a twenty-five-year-old whose idea of sophisticated was a clean pair of jeans and Swiss cheese on his hamburger.

She was probably interested in designer clothes and upscale dining with impeccable service and two-hundred-dollar bottles of wine. They probably got a suite in the most expensive hotel in the city.

Time to face facts. Letti Aldrete was so far out of his league it wasn't funny.

Kevin felt stupid to be so disappointed.

He snapped off the lights in the concession stand and was about to go home and lick his wounds when Josh Goldstein and Rachel Castillo, the executive and artistic directors, came out of the theater. They were accompanied by Jessica and a tall young man with brilliant red hair and a smile on his face. Jessica introduced the man as Brian.

"We're all headed down the street to Thirties to talk smack, eat bar food, and throw back a few," Josh said. "Care to join us?"

Kevin looked at their youthful faces, all contemporaries, and nodded. These people were more his speed.

"Beer and chicken wings? Count me in."

Chapter Five

Letti's date was disappointed. She could see it in his eyes.

And sex appeal? He wasn't bad, but Kevin had him beat hands down.

She let Diego Rodriguez escort her to the black Lexus parked in front of the dry cleaner's across the street. He had been waiting in the lobby, apparently impatient. The minute he spotted her, his face had fallen and it had been all she could do not to turn on her heel and go out the back.

But his smile had been friendly as he'd introduced himself. "I normally refuse to go on blind dates," he said. "But you sounded so lovely when Sonia described you, I decided to make an exception."

"Thank you." *I think.*

He seated her in the expensive car and asked if an upscale seafood restaurant on the Riverwalk was okay. "Every San Antonio cliché in the book. I know. But I do love it down on the river," he said.

"And I love that restaurant," Letti told him, feeling herself perk up. Maybe tonight wasn't going to be so bad after all.

"And then we can catch some music at El Rio Rojo or one of the other clubs on the river. Does that work for you?"

That worked for her just fine. They made small talk during the short drive. The night was balmy and a half-moon hung over the river as they walked down the wide staircase to the river level, one story down from the street. Bright lights twinkled from the trees and neon signs announced the restaurants and shops lining the banks. The sidewalk was thick with tourists and locals, mostly couples and groups of adults. The sidewalk tables were filled with drinkers and diners, and music drifted from the bars and restaurants.

Diego escorted her to the seafood restaurant and gave his name to the host. They were immediately escorted to an outdoor table near the water. Letti sank back in her chair and let the ambiance surround her. "I love it down here," she said as she opened her menu. "And I especially enjoy the food here. Good choice."

Diego's eyes twinkled. "I may have had a little help. Sonia said your mother mentioned that you especially liked this one."

Wow. Points for that big time. Letti perked up even more. If he cared enough to find out where she liked to eat, he must want this date to go well.

Maybe some things were more important than sex appeal.

They perused the menu and made their choices. Diego was a practiced raconteur and before the waiter had come to take their orders, Diego had her engaged in a lively discussion of the San Antonio entertainment scene. She wasn't surprised to learn he loved live theater. Who didn't? But she was surprised to learn they both had a weakness for well-performed jazz and mariachi, and that Diego had paid for a good bit of his college education playing guitarron in a mariachi band. That sent their conversation in the direction of mariachi bands in general, and they had fun dredging up the old gossip around the drug bust involving a mariachi band out of El Rio Rojo and a couple of the Navarro heirs.

It seemed they had gossiping in common as well.

Their platters of fish arrived and they fell silent but for oohs and aahs as they savored the delicious seafood. He asked her about her acting and she regaled him with stories of her years in California, and the productions she'd done in the community theaters in and around San Antonio. To her delight, he remembered a couple of the musicals she'd performed in.

"It's been a long time since I saw the *How to Succeed in Business without Really Trying* in the Boerne Theater," he said. "But I remember it was good. And that the J. Pierrepont Finch actor was particularly talented."

"That was my ex," Letti said dryly. "I'll give him your regards."

"Oops. Sorry about that."

They both laughed. Conversation continued, to art and politics and community affairs. Diego was easy to talk to, and she was surprised by how many interests they had in common. The waiter cleared the table and Diego paid for dinner. And still they lingered, as the crowd thinned and the moon dipped lower in the sky. Letti was charmed by this delightful man.

He was a winner in every way.

Finally he rose and drew her to her feet. "Thank you for a lovely meal," she said.

"No, thank you. I haven't had such stimulating dinner conversation in a long time. I wish I could have them more often."

"That's easy," Letti said. "Ask me back out. We could cover religion and child-rearing next time. That would make for some really interesting discussion."

"I-I doubt that will happen." He looked at her with an unfathomable expression. "I wish—" he stopped and shrugged his shoulders ruefully.

Letti's lips tightened. "You wish what?" she prompted.

"I wish you were about ten years younger."

Letti stiffened. "What does my age have to do with dinner table conversation?"

Diego sighed. "Sonia wasn't completely honest with your mother. I've played the field and enjoyed the ladies for twenty-five years and I'm finally ready to settle down and raise a family. I'm looking for a woman who's also ready to get married, but still young enough to have a family with me. Someone who wants to have my children. Not an older—I mean, not a woman who's already raised her family."

"And you didn't realize how old I was or you would have never called," Letti finished.

"True. But I am glad I called and I am glad we got to have the evening together."

Big fucking whoop. Disappointment reared up and smacked her in the face. "I enjoyed it too, for all the good it did either of us. I guess you better get me back to my car. It's parked in the lot behind the theater."

"You don't want to listen to the music at Rio Rojo?"

"Not particularly. You don't need to waste any more time with me. You need to get out there and find your brood mare, and I need to get home and wash my dentures and rub my arthritic knees with Ben Gay."

Diego's eyes narrowed. "If that's what you want."

"That's exactly what I want. Time's a-wastin', buddy. You better get on with it and find her before your hair and your teeth fall out."

"You don't have to be snarky," he said stiffly. "Would you rather I'd ghosted you?"

"I'd rather you weren't a prick."

They were silent on the way back to the theater. As they drove past Thirties, Letti spotted a familiar figure with sun-streaked hair coming out the door. He seemed steady enough on his feet, but something about the way he was moving set off alarm bells in her head. She hoped the cab by the curb was his, but another couple got in the taxi and he started toward the Durango parking lot.

She directed Diego to the parking lot in the back and got out of the car before he had the engine off. "Tell your sister she needs to be a little more specific the next time she fixes you up with a date," she said tersely as she slammed his car door.

Diego's face was grim as he pulled out of the parking lot. She started to go home, but decided to wait and make sure Kevin was sober enough to drive. He wandered into the lot a couple of minutes later, where she waited by his car with her arms crossed in front of her.

"Whoa, beautiful. Whatcha doin' here? Where's lover boy?" he asked as he bobbed his eyebrows up and down.

"My date dropped me off here at the car. I waited to make sure you're sober enough to drive. Which, from the way you're swaying back and forth, I'd have to say you aren't."

He grinned impudently. "Mrs. Aldrete, your perception of the obvious is outstanding. Absolutely outstanding." He put his fist to his stomach and belched. "I figured that out about halfway down the sidewalk. Do you know that the Fruteria sign dances up and down this time of night?"

"Good lord, Kevin. How much did you have to drink?"

"More than I shoulda, I guess."

"How in the hell were you planning to get home? And for god sakes, I'm Letti. Mrs. Aldrete's my mother-in-law."

"Besides, I've seen you naked." His eyes danced.

"Don't remind me," she said through clenched teeth. "Go ahead, get in the damned car. I'll take you home."

She clicked open the crossover and half-pushed Kevin into the passenger seat. "Where do you live?"

He gave her an address in tony Alamo Heights. She set her GPS for the fifteen-minute drive and pulled out of the parking lot. "Who was at Thirties with you? Do they need a ride?"

Kevin looked at the roof of the car. "Josh and Rachel were still there. Said they'd get an Uber when they wanted to leave. Jessica and her redheaded cop left early. Prob'ly went home to fuck."

"Aww. They got back together. I'm glad."

"I thought you were mad at Jessica."

"I am. I can be mad at her and happy for her at the same time."

"Okay. If you say so." He burped again, beer fumes filling the car.

She wrinkled her nose. "What did you do? Drink half the brewery?"

"I was all upset. You had a date. The beer made it better."

She stopped at a red light. "Wait. You went out and got drunk because I had a date? That's ridiculous." She ignored the little thrill that shot through her.

He was jealous. Well, what do you know?

The light turned green and she took the left that would lead her into Alamo Heights.

"It's not ridiculous," he protested. "That guy. He has money and he's slick. He takes you to fancy restaurants and buys you fancy wine, and he wouldn't need any tutoring." He crossed his arms in front of him. "Of course, you'd rather go out with him."

Letti's lips twitched. "Do you always whine when you're drunk?"

He thought a minute. "Prob'ly."

She bit her lip to keep from laughing.

They pulled into the curving driveway of the address he'd given her and she eyed the sprawling two-story stone house. "My god. No wonder your parents can afford to be so generous with the theater," she breathed. "I knew they had money, but I had no idea they were this well off."

Kevin shrugged. "It's just home to me. Sort of. I'm living in the carriage house apartment in the back."

"The old servants' quarters," Letti murmured.

"Mom and Dad use it as a guest house. They said I could live out there while I'm in law school." She put the car in park and he turned to face her. "So how was your date with Mr. Sophication?"

"Don't you mean sophistication?"

"I mean your rich lover boy."

Letti's mood plummeted at the reminder. "In a word, it sucked. He was a douchebag of the highest order."

Kevin's eyes widened. "What happened? Do I need to beat the shit outta him for you?"

"I was too old for the bastard. The dick came out and told me he wished I was ten years younger. He's looking for a young wife to make him a passel of kids. I'm about ten years past my expiration date."

Kevin's eyes widened. "Wow. He's an asshole."

Letti shrugged. "But he's right. I'm not what he's looking for."

"That's bullshit." His eyes blazed in the dim light of the streetlamp. "You may not be what he thinks he wants, but I promise you, Letti, you're not old."

"Yeah, right. But thanks for saying so."

"It's true. How 'bout I prove it to you?"

Before she quite knew what happened, Kevin curved his arm around her neck and pulled her to him across the narrow console. His lips crashed down on hers, firm and tender at the same time as he took immediate possession of her mouth.

At first she was too stunned to do anything but let him kiss her. But shock gave way to pleasure as her dormant senses came alive as they had the last time she'd been in his arms.

The touch and taste of his lips, flavored with beer, the warmth of his hands, the scent of his shampoo and his aftershave, and the essence that was uniquely Kevin electrified her lips, her breasts, and between her legs, touching her in a way no other lover had.

Her breath hitched as she opened her lips to him, inviting him into her mouth. Her heart raced and the blood pounded in her ears as his tongue dueled with hers.

Chills raced down her back. She reached out and fisted the soft fabric of his tee shirt, pulling him as close as he could come given the console between them.

Dear god. Had a kiss ever made her feel this way?

Kevin's had. It'd been five years, but her body remembered his, and responded to his touch. Kevin made her come alive again, and made her body sing.

He shifted in his seat. Her fingers dug into his arms as he palmed her breasts through her sweater, his touch barely there as he coaxed her nipples into hard, aching nubs. For long moments he touched her and she let herself savor his fingers on her body. Her hands crept up his arms to the muscles in his shoulders, warm and hard and strong. He was noticeably broader than he'd been their first time. He'd been a boy then. Now he was all man.

Kevin broke the kiss. "Did I make my point?"

Letti blinked. "Huh? What?"

"You still think you're old, or do I need to kiss you again to make my point?"

"I kind of think you did."

"I'm not done with you. Kissing you was everything. I meant what I said the other day. I'd love to be inside you again. You could give me another lesson or two."

"I don't think you need any more tutoring." A wave of affection for him rolled over her and she held his face in her hands. "You're a sweetheart. I haven't felt this good in a damned long time. But. Right now you're wearing a thick pair of beer goggles. Let's see how eager you are to take me to bed when you're sober and can see the laugh lines at the corners of my eyes."

Kevin's eyes smoldered as he stared across the console. "It's not the beer. I promise. It's you. Gimme your phone."

She handed him her phone and he typed in his number and hit send. His phone pinged a second later. "There. I'll text you in the morning." He handed her the phone and kissed her once more, quick and hard, and then slid out of the car.

Letti watched him disappear through a side gate. She touched her finger to her still-throbbing lips. Damn, even if he didn't want her in the morning, he had managed to soothe the sting of Diego's rejection, replacing it with a healthy dose of lust, and an admitted boost to her battered ego.

Kevin probably wouldn't want her in the morning, she told herself as she backed out of the driveway. He'd sober up and see her for the forty-year-old woman that she was, and realize he didn't want her.

But it sure would be a lot of fun if he did.

Chapter Six

Kevin stared across the bed at her, his eyes smoldering as he took her in. "You're beautiful, Letti. So beautiful." He reached out and ran his hand down her side, from her breast to her hip. "Beautiful and sexy."

Letti touched the tangled hair on his chest. "You're mine. All mine." She moved closer to him and he wrapped her in his arms and gave her a long, languorous kiss that seemed to go on forever. "Make love to me, Kevin. I want you inside me again."

He rolled to his back, his erection rising from his body, and beckoned to her. "Ride me, Letti. I want to see you above me when we make love."

She threw her leg across his hips and rose up, easing her body down on his as they came together. Kevin reached up and turned her face toward the large dresser mirror. The soft light of morning filtering through the shades bathed their young, perfect bodies in a golden glow. Their youthful faces were portraits of passion and joy. "Look at her making love to me. Isn't she the most beautiful girl you've ever seen?"

Twenty-five-year-old Letti smiled as she moved in his arms.

Letti blinked in the early morning dimness of her big, lonely bedroom. Something, she wasn't sure what, had interrupted her dream-filled slumber. It wasn't all that early, but the thick shades and drapes assured her almost night-like darkness for as long as she wanted it. Her breasts were heavy and she throbbed between her legs as her dream teased the edges of her mind, and made her body cry out for his touch. Her hand slid down her stomach and under the elastic of her short pajama bottoms, sliding down to her sweet spot and touching herself until the memory of the dream coupled with her own desire had her exploding.

The immediate need assuaged, she turned on her side and stared at the big dresser mirror where she'd seen herself making love to

Kevin. He'd told her to look at herself. He'd said she was the most beautiful girl he'd ever seen.

Letti's eyes stung with unshed tears at the image she'd seen in the dream mirror. The fresh face, the firm body, the smooth skin around her eyes and mouth.

She shut her eyes and groaned and wondered what had made her wake up this early. That question was answered a moment later when her phone pinged, she guessed for the second time this morning. She was tempted to ignore it, but it might be a problem with her grandmother, or with Marco. She picked up the phone and held it out away from her face to read the message.

Sober as a judge and ready for my next lesson. When and where?

He accompanied the text with a heart emoji.

Her lips twitched.

He still wanted her.

She didn't know if that pleased her or not.

Either way, she wasn't falling back to sleep.

She curled up, not yet ready to get up and face the world. Hell of a note. The age-appropriate man she'd had so much in common with hadn't wanted her. The twenty-five-year-old with whom she had almost nothing in common did. The attraction that exploded to life every time she and Kevin were in the same room made absolutely no sense. But he wanted another go, and she was seriously considering it.

Maybe other things *weren't* as important as sex appeal.

Which Kevin had in spades.

She wasn't all that sure it was true for her.

Giving up on getting any more sleep, she padded downstairs to the kitchen and made a cup of coffee, which she carried back upstairs to her bathroom. A long shower and the coffee did a lot to revive her. She toweled herself dry and blotted the water from her hair before running a wide-toothed comb through it. The rich dark brown was a close match to her original color and her colorist was the best in town. Few people knew it wasn't her own any more.

But she knew. And it bothered her.

The entire aging process bothered her.

She leaned forward and stared in the mirror at her naked body and unadorned face. The dream once again drove home the fact that she would never ever be that young girl making love to Kevin. It wasn't as if she was a troll. She knew she was good-looking. Always had been, always would be. Genetics gave her the goods. She kept up the maintenance. Her body was always curvy, more so after she had children. But, she took care of herself, and ate carefully. There was no help for gravity unless she had "work" done, and she wasn't there yet, but in five years, she might be.

Regardless of the creams, lotions, serums, hair dye, and over-priced conditioner, the bloom was off the rose. The freshness of youth was gone, and had been for some time. Her skin lacked the elasticity of a younger woman's, and unless she wore stage make-up, a dewy complexion was never happening again.

Her breasts were no longer perky without a bra. Thanks to her faithful exercise routine, her stomach was mostly flat, but two pregnancies had graced her with stretch marks. Despite the prescription Retin-A, laugh lines were becoming more than faint at the corner of her eyes.

A lot of the changes were subtle and individually no big deal, but taken together, her age showed. Nobody in their right mind would mistake her for a twenty-five-year-old. In dim light with a great makeup job, she might pass for thirty. With her normal makeup and a good night's sleep, she could do thirty-five.

But in the harsh light of her bathroom, naked and scrubbed free of makeup, she looked every day of her forty years. A beautiful forty, but still forty.

Kevin had to be out of his mind.

She was out of hers too, for wanting him.

Whatever.

She unearthed a pair of black knit slacks and a pretty knit shirt that would pass muster at Mass, and still be dark enough backstage. Sophie was already in the kitchen with a glass of orange juice and two pieces of toast in front of her. Letti looked at the toast doubtfully. "Is that going to hold you?"

"I'll be fine. Doug's mom's getting pizza for lunch before we start working on the design."

"That's nice of her. She's been a good sport about hosting that club in her home."

"She has. But she's hinted a few times that she'd like some of the other moms to open their homes. Can I invite the group over here? We have Daddy's old man cave we hardly use any more."

Letti sighed. "Yet another obligation when you need to be concentrating on the theater."

Sophie's eyes narrowed. "Tell me. If I'd asked to have the theater kids over, what would you have said? Would you have said it was another obligation, or would you have given me your immediate approval with a big fat smile on your face?"

Busted. "I would have given you the nod," she answered slowly.

"That's what I thought. So what's the difference? Theater kids in the man cave, or engineering kids in the man cave?"

"Fine. Do what you want," Letti said stiffly. "But you have so much more in common with the theater kids than those in the engineering club. Now, changing the subject. Have you downloaded the applications to USC and Yale yet? Lots of seriously famous actors went through Yale. Meryl Streep and Jodi Foster, to name a couple."

"No, I haven't." Sophie took a bite of her toast.

"Why not?" Letti demanded.

"Haven't got that far. Besides, they aren't due for months yet. None of them are. I'll have all summer and into the fall to work on them."

"That may be, but it would help if we had hard copies of them now so we could look them over and at least know what they're looking for."

"We know what they're looking for. Gobs of acting and theater experience. Straight As, loads of extracurricular activities, and enough community service to save the world. None of which I've lived up to."

"You've come pretty damned close," Letti said.

"Okay, Mom, I have plenty of time. Chill."

"I will not chill. By the time you get home from your engineering thing, I will have the list of schools from which you need to download the applications. It's going to take time, to do them all, and we need to get started early."

"Quit pushing me," Sophie said tightly. "That's all you know how to do. You push me and push everybody else around you. I am *tired* of being pushed. I said I'd take care of it this summer and I will." She shoved the rest of the toast in her mouth. "I'm going on to early Mass. I need to be over to Doug's by noon." She jumped up and stalked out before Letti could respond.

Well, hell. Sophie thought her mother was pushy. Of course she was. She had to be. It didn't matter what Sophie's dream was, there were only so many slots in the top schools, and fewer financial assistance offerings. Letti got Sophie was a kid, but she had to be realistic. No dream came true only because you wanted it to. You had to work for it. All day, every day.

Letti picked up her car keys and headed out the door. Now she could expect a grilling regarding her date last night. She was in no mood to sugarcoat the disaster. She would tell her mother and grandmother exactly what happened in one syllable words, and she dared them to try to fix her up with somebody else again after last night's fiasco.

Letti's lips twitched. Well, maybe she wouldn't tell them everything that had gone on last night. They didn't need to know that a twenty-five-year-old had kissed her stupid and wanted to be inside her again. They sure didn't need to know how tempted Letti was to take him up on his offer. Her mother would be shocked and her grandmother would have a heart attack and die on the spot.

To their credit, her mother and grandmother waited until mass was over and they were sharing Mom's tasty *migas* before broaching the subject. "Wasn't your date with Diego Rodriguez last night?" Mom asked innocently.

"It was," Letti said tightly.

"*Como estuvo*? How was it? *Te divertiste*? Is he as *guapo* as Sonia says? Are you going back out with him?" *Abuela* asked eagerly.

"In a nutshell, it was great until it wasn't. So no, I didn't have a good time. Yes, he's good looking and no, I won't be going out with him again. Now, let's talk about something more pleasant than last night's date. Something fun. Like global warming or the war in the Middle East."

Their eyes widened. "*Que paso?*" her grandmother demanded.

"What happened?" Mom echoed. "Was he boring? Did he drink too much? Did he try something?"

"No, he wasn't boring. He was quite charming, in fact." Letti lifted her chin. "We talked about anything and everything and discovered that we have a lot in common. Had the time of our lives. And then he told me he won't be asking me out again because he's looking for a young wife to give him kids, and that if he'd known how old I am, he wouldn't have bothered calling."

Her mother and grandmother's faces fell. "*Lo siento*, Letti," her grandmother murmured. "I'm sorry he hurt your feelings."

"What a *pendejo*," Mom added. "I'll make sure Sonia hears about it."

"Why bother?" Letti asked. "It is what it is."

"I'll do a little better next time," her mother said.

"Mom. There will not be a next time. I am done with blind dates, yours or anybody else's. You and *Abuelita* will have to suffer the shame of having a divorced, middle-aged daughter in the family."

"Letti."

"*No, Abuelita*. No more blind dates. I'm done."

"All right. All right." Mom threw up her hands. "I hear you. After that, I don't blame you."

"Besides, how does he know I'm past having children?" Letti asked.

"He doesn't. But you probably are," Mom said quietly. "The women in our family tend to have early menopause. I was only forty-two."

"I was forty," *Abuela* added.

Letti thought a minute. She hadn't had a period in two months. Or was it three? She'd been busy and with no reason to worry about pregnancy, she hadn't thought about it one way or the other. But there it was. Diego had been right.

"Not that it matters," Mom said briskly. "There are plenty of older men out there who already have families who aren't going to expect you to have children. Maybe that's the direction we need to think."

"'We' aren't thinking anything," Letti snapped. "I already told you. No more blind dates. Especially no blind dates with the fifty-something crowd."

"That's exactly the direction you should be thinking," Mom argued. "You would be young to a fifty-year-old."

"No way. I don't want some old fart with a medicine cabinet full of little blue pills."

That would be as bad as playing an older role at the Durango.

"Letti, a young man's not going to want you," *Abuela* said imperiously.

Wanna bet? Letti bit her tongue before she could tell her grandmother that's exactly who wanted her. Her grandmother would be scandalized.

Instead, Letti shook her head. "I would rather be alone than settle for some old man because he'd have me."

"No *importa*. Never mind." Her grandmother sighed. "You don't care what we think."

That was the damned truth.

They finished their lunch and Letti made her getaway. The entire morning had her grinding her teeth. Sophie dragging her feet on the applications. Her mother and grandmother's obsession with her getting married again. The suggestion that she think about older men as the best option. That one really pissed her off. She wasn't that damned old.

Especially if a man as young as Kevin wanted her. Wanted to sleep with her. Wanted to fuck her.

The thought was tempting in the extreme.

The Durango's back door was locked and she used her key to let herself in. The theater was deserted. In her haste to get away from her mother and grandmother, she'd arrived a good hour before she'd needed to. She went through her pre-performance chores, and finding herself way ahead of schedule, escaped to her favorite hidey-hole, the deserted balcony. She sat in the first row and checked her email, reading a few and deleting. She was going through the last of them when her phone pinged and a message popped up on the screen.

Another lesson?

Letti stared down at the screen. Why the hell not? He wanted her. She wanted him. The mere thought a man his age desired her was a turn-on in the extreme. Her battered ego could sure use the boost. If the sex was anywhere near as good as she remembered, it would be a lot of fun.

The best thing about it: nothing would ever come of it. They would take a moment out of time, have their fun, and go on their merry way.

Letti felt the slightest pang at the thought, but common sense said this would be to work off the edge, have great sex, and nothing more. They needed to talk to make sure they were on the same page and good with it. She stared down at the screen for a minute before her fingers started flying.

We'll talk after the show.

She smiled and put her phone away.

It was about time she had a little fun, and a few nights in Kevin's bed would be a stupendous way to do it.

Chapter Seven

Kevin swallowed the last of his coffee and rubbed his aching temples. "Have fun last night?" his father asked with a smirk.

"Too much," he admitted. "Those craft beers pack a punch."

"Oh d-dear," his mother said. "You d-drove home l-like that?"

Kevin shook his head, wincing at the pain. "No. I had someone drive me." A thought crossed his mind. His parents' bedroom windows faced the street and looked right down into the circular driveway. If they'd been looking out, they would have had a ringside seat of him laying a hot wet one on Letti. That would be fun to explain.

But their curtains had been drawn, and his parents went to bed early, so it was doubtful they'd seen what he and Letti had been up to.

But still.

He carried his coffee cup to the coffeemaker and put in another pod. It was going to take at least three cups before he felt human. That and a text from a certain sexy lady taking him up on his offer. He'd heard nothing yet, but that didn't have him worried. He would see her this afternoon at the theater and continue to press her then.

He felt his lips curve into a smile at the thought.

His mother was serving him another spoonful of eggs as he sat back down. "H-here. You n-need to eat. You won't g-g-get to eat until s-supper."

He smiled gratefully. "Thanks." He looked around. "Is Emma sleeping in?"

"She is. I'm not taking her home until late in the afternoon. I don't care if it makes her asshole father mad," Dad said.

His mother looked at him with a troubled expression. "S-she asked us l-last n-night if-if she c-could move in wh-when she t-turns eight-teen."

"I hope you told her yes," Kevin said. "The bastard stank like cheap booze at nine in the morning."

"Of course she can," Dad said. "It breaks my heart that she has to, though. It's not what her mother would have wanted for her, or for her asshole father."

"It's what needs to happen. God knows what kind of verbal abuse he subjects her to," Kevin said hotly.

"I h-hate th-that f-for my only g-grandchild," Barbara said. "You n-need to find a n-nice g-girl t-to m-marry. W-with R-renee gone, you're m-my only chance f-for m-more grandch-children. I c-could introd-duce you to a f-few of my friends' g-granddaughters."

"Mom, we've had this discussion. I want to give you those grandchildren someday. More than you could know. One of my dearest dreams and half of why I gave up on LA and came home is because I knew the likelihood of finding someone to marry and have kids with there was slim. But, and this is a big but, I'm looking at three years of law school and establishing a practice before I can even think about the obligations of a family. I want a family. I want one with all my heart. But not now."

Besides, if he was out looking for the nice girl his mother wanted for him, he wouldn't be free to pursue the forty-year-old hottie he kissed the hell out of last night.

"J-just d-don't wait t-too long. Your f-father and I aren't g-getting any young-ger."

That was true. There were fifteen years between him and his late sister, and his parents had both been on the high side of forty when he was born. Still, he wouldn't marry and start a family only to please his mother. He would settle down with a wife and kids on his timetable, not hers. His mom was simply going to have to be patient.

While he had his fling with a sexy forty-year-old.

Letti's car was already in the theater parking lot. He pulled in beside her and let himself in the back door. He looked around, but she was nowhere to be seen. He loaded the popcorn machine and ran a quick vacuum over the carpet. The bathrooms needed a bit of freshening up. He was running a brush around the toilet in the ladies room when his phone pinged and a text popped onto the screen.

We'll talk after the show.

Pillow talk? Worked for him.

After the bathrooms, he organized the will-call tickets. He still hadn't seen Letti. Suddenly he needed to. The question was where to find her. There were plenty of dark places in the theater for a person to hang out, and surely she had one. She wasn't in the ticket room off the lobby. He checked the downstairs closet and found it locked. The stairs were cordoned off, but one of the stands had been moved over a smidgen. A-ha. He'd bet his next paycheck Letti had escaped to the balcony for a few minutes of privacy.

Privacy that begged to be invaded.

He slipped through the ropes and took the stairs two at a time. Letti was seated in the front row, her legs propped on the railing and her feet crossed at the ankles. He loped down the risers and plunked down beside her.

A small smile touched her lips as she turned to him. "Did you wake up with a hangover?"

"I've had worse. Three cups of coffee and Mom's southern scrambled eggs worked wonders."

"Southern scrambled eggs? Never heard of such a thing."

"She scrambles them with thick cream, and sprinkles them with chives."

"Sounds good." She looked at him curiously. "No cook?"

Kevin laughed. "They have money, but not that much. Besides, Mom loves cooking. A cook's the last person she'd hire. So what did you have for breakfast?"

"*Migas* and an inquisition. I told my mother to lay off the blind dates."

He ran his hand up her arm. "Did you tell her why?"

Letti looked at him and burst out laughing. "Yeah, right. I'm going to tell my mother and my pious grandmother I've got the hots for a twenty-five-year-old."

He felt his body tighten and the blood rush to his cock. "Do you? Have the hots for a twenty-five-year-old?"

"No. I was humoring you last night," she snarked. "Jesus, Kevin. Yeah, I have the hots for you. Why do you think I told you we'd talk after the show?"

"I don't know. I thought you might want to talk about the weather or something."

Letti rolled her eyes. "A comedian you're not." She looked down and sat up straight. "Damn. I see kids on the stage. I better get down there."

"So had I." He took her by the hand and they climbed the steep stairs to the top of the balcony. "Wait a minute." He glanced around and found a spot behind the sound booth that was invisible to anyone looking up into the balcony. "If I don't kiss you at least once, I'm not gonna make it through the afternoon."

He pressed her against the wall and took her into his arms. Her lips were open and moist as he took possession of her mouth. Her arms wrapped around his waist and she yanked him closer, so they were plastered together from their heads to their knees.

Her tongue danced with his as they fought a sensual duel. The hardened tips of her soft breasts dug into his chest and his rapidly swelling cock poked her stomach. She smelled of herbal shampoo and fresh fabric, and the unique essence that he remembered from their one night together, a heady scent that was inexplicably erotic.

Desire twisted his gut as his hands ran down her back and gripped her butt, pulling her up into his body. His breath hitched in his throat. Blood pounded in his ears as their lips and tongues nipped and nibbled and explored.

The clothing barrier was frustrating, and he hoped it would be gone later this evening.

They kissed for long moments. When he raised his head and looked down, her lips were swollen and her eyes were glazed. "Damn, woman. You look good enough to eat."

She looked at the bulge in his jeans. "You look pretty kissed yourself," she said dryly. "Better adjust your pants before you go out in the lobby." She reached up and ran her hand down his face. "We'll talk after the show."

Hopefully they would do more than talk.

She ran her fingers through her hair and disappeared into the stairwell. He gave her a few minutes and followed her down. He was still at half-mast, but his jeans were loose enough that it didn't show.

Today was the middle school production, which Rachel had explained involved fewer families, but more of the performers' friends. Soon the lobby was filled with enthusiastic thirteen-year-olds.

The afternoon crawled by. He managed a few minutes to slip in and see part of the performance, but he couldn't have said if it was good or terrible. His mind kept drifting back to that kiss in the balcony, and he would start to get hard all over again.

Finally, the show was over and the cast was in the lobby, shaking hands and accepting congratulations. He wasted no time shutting down the concession and cleaning the lobby and was leaning against Letti's crossover and sweating a little when she came out the back door. She raised her eyebrow as she headed straight to her car.

"Still interested?" she asked.

"Would I be standing out here in the hot sun waiting for you if I weren't?" He glanced around. "I guess this is kind of public."

"So? I do theater, you do theater. We know one another. I doubt anyone's going to suspect we're anything but acquaintances."

That didn't sit well. "Why? Is the thought of you and me getting together that preposterous?"

"To us, maybe not. To the rest of humanity, probably. Not that I'm into pleasing the rest of humanity." She handed him a small piece of paper with an address he'd never heard of. "Put that in your GPS in case we get separated. We can have an early dinner and talk. Don't look so disappointed," she added when his face fell. "We'll talk. It'll be fine."

Kevin got in the car and put the address in his GPS. He wasn't sure why they had to talk. In his world, if he and a woman wanted to hook up, they hooked up. But maybe that was the way older couples did things, discussing everything first.

Shoving his disappointment aside, he followed her out of the parking lot and onto the expressway. She was a fast driver, but he managed to keep up with her as she drove past downtown and took an exit near Mission San Jose. He followed her south, past the famous old mission into a part of town totally unfamiliar to him. The houses and businesses had definitely seen better days. He wondered why she wanted to come over here. Maybe it was her old stomping ground or something. She finally pulled into the parking lot of a rundown strip mall and parked in front of a small restaurant advertising 'The Best Hamburgers on the South Side.'

He certainly hoped so.

He pulled in beside her and followed her inside. Most of the tables were unoccupied, which wasn't surprising on a Sunday afternoon at five. The waitress didn't appear to recognize Letti and showed them to a booth in the corner. They slid in across from one another and opened their menus.

"Why here?" he asked as the waitress walked away. "Your old neighborhood?"

"Nah. I found out about this place from one of my students a couple of years ago. I came here because the burgers are to die for. And there is less than a zero chance that we'll run into someone that we know."

"I thought we weren't into pleasing the rest of humanity."

"We're not. But I don't want to have to explain myself to anybody either. And the burgers really are delicious. Particularly the one with refried beans and jalapenos in the melted cheese."

"Ah. A hamburger after my own heart."

The waitress returned and they ordered the jalapeno burgers and big sodas. Letti folded her hands in front of her and leaned forward. "Before we start anything, I want to make sure we're on the same page." She took a breath. "A weekend or two, maybe a couple of months. Something light. Something fun. Nothing serious."

Kevin nodded. "Works for me." He ignored the little pang of disappointment that it couldn't be more and reminded himself that he was in no position to do serious. He grinned impudently. "So whatcha doing after hamburgers tonight?"

"Grading a bunch of papers and making sure Sophie's downloaded the college applications I told her to," she said. "Also supervising Marco's homework when he gets back from his dad's house. It's not like I can drop everything and have a booty call, as tempting as that might be."

"I hadn't thought of that. When can we get together?"

Letti thought a minute. "Owen has both kids next weekend. I'm overseeing the crewing for the teenage production next Friday night, but the minute that's over I'm free for the weekend."

"Me, too. Do we shoot for the whole weekend?"

"Won't your parents wonder where you are?"

"I come and go as I please. Out of courtesy, I'll tell Mom I'm spending the weekend away, but I won't volunteer more than that, and Mom won't ask. She's gotten used to the idea that I'm an adult."

"No, she hasn't. She only acts like she has." Letti grinned. "Moms never stop wondering where their kids are."

"What are you going to tell yours?"

"Mom or kids?"

"Both."

"I'll probably tell them all the same thing. That I'm behind on my grading and plan to spend the entire weekend playing catch-up. It's happened often enough for real that none of them will think anything of it. Let's shoot for the whole weekend. I'd love that."

"So would I. We can decide where we want to go later in the week." Anyplace would work for him as long as he could get Letti naked, but he wasn't about to tell her that. Besides, she was most likely used to nice places, and if he was going to keep up with Diego the asshole, he was going to have to up his game.

The waitress brought their sodas. Kevin's smile was big as he slurped his. "Big Red. I missed those in California. That and Shiner Blonde."

She pointed at the soda. "You can keep the sugary soda, but I get your point about Shiner Blonde. My personal favorite is Corona, but Shiner Blonde's a close second."

"Not a margarita lady?"

"Those work too. I'm surprised you missed anything about Texas. I would have thought you'd have loved everything about LA. I sure did."

"Really? When were you in California?" He knew the answer but didn't want her to know he'd talked about her.

"I got my first degree from USC. That's where I met Owen. We were both acting majors. I loved USC and I loved LA, even the parts other people hate, like the crowds and the traffic. I was totally prepared to spend the rest of my life there. I was going to take LA by storm and make my fame and fortune in the entertainment industry."

"TV and movies?"

"That's what I wanted. Not that I have a thing against stage work. Obviously."

"Obviously. So what happened?"

She smiled ruefully. "Do the math. I'm forty. Sophie turns eighteen this year. I got pregnant my senior year. There went fame and fortune."

"Why? Plenty of the women I worked with had kids."

"Those women were established and earned enough to pay for childcare. They weren't living the hardscrabble, hand-to-mouth existence beginners and wannabes live. As much as I wanted it for myself, I couldn't do that to my child."

He looked at her curiously. "You never considered an abortion?"

"No. Never." Letti's eyes flashed. "I loved Sophie from the minute I found out about her. Which may seem strange, considering the one-hundred-eighty-degree turnaround I had to make in my life and career path."

"It doesn't seem strange to me you would love your child."

"Thank you for understanding. Not everybody does. Thank god Owen felt the same way. We got married the weekend after graduation and came back here to a support system. Dad got Owen into the police academy and my grandmother kept Sophie so I could commute to Texas State for my MFA in directing."

"Then what?"

"I went to work for the local junior college. I had Marco. Owen went to work as a police officer. We fed our acting addiction at the community theaters around town. Even did a few in Boerne. I thought everything was great, and I was happy enough. At least until the divorce, and I'd like to think I've gotten past that and gone on. But I've never, ever gotten over feeling like I missed out, that the ship sailed without me." She sipped her soda. "It hurts sometimes."

"I'm sorry it gets to you."

"I'm all right with it most of the time. But occasionally, it all piles up on me. Like the afternoon I found out Emma was cast as Ariel instead of Sophie. If I hadn't just found out that I'd been passed over, I wouldn't have reacted so negatively. But Rachel asked me to be crew chief, again, and then Sophie told me she'd also been overlooked and I was loaded for bear. I get tired of losing good roles, and then to do it to Sophie—it was too much."

Kevin felt his lips twitch. "Has anybody pointed out to you that Ariel is a girl?"

Letti's expression tightened. "You think dumbass questions like that are going to further your cause in getting laid?"

"Uh, well, no." Kevin felt his face turn red. "Do they overlook you often?"

"All the damn time." Her tone was bitter.

"That's sad. There are a lot of good roles out there you'd be perfect in. But are you interested in playing any of them?"

Letti raised her eyebrow. "What roles? You think I want to play somebody's mother? Or grandmother?"

"Not...not grandmother," he stammered.

"I'm not interested in playing somebody's middle-aged mother, either."

Okay, if he kept on he was going to make her really mad. "I'm sorry they don't want you for the roles you want to play," he said softly.

"It is what it is."

Kevin wanted to say more but bit his lip. He wanted to push his case, try to convince her to take some of those older roles. She would be wonderful in them. But he'd be damned if he'd make her mad by telling her so.

The waitress picked that moment to deliver two delicious-smelling burgers.

Letti bit into hers and moaned.

"Good?" he asked.

She nodded and gestured for him to do the same. One bite had his taste buds dancing with joy. It was the perfect blend of gooey melted cheese, spicy jalapenos and cold *pico de gallo*.

He watched Letti eat as he savored his own burger. She ate with enthusiasm, not starving herself to stay thin, her pleasure in the burger evident with each bite she took. It was almost a sensual experience watching her devour the massive concoction. Her lips curving around the bun. The delight on her face as she chewed and swallowed. Her obvious enjoyment in the savory treat.

It was the first time in his life he'd gotten a hard-on watching a woman eat.

He shifted slightly in his seat and concentrated on his own food, each bite exploding with flavor. It didn't take either of them long to polish off the burgers and the salty, crispy fries. The waitress took their empty baskets and topped off their sodas.

Letti sipped her drink and looked at him quizzically. "So what did you think of California, other than missing Big Red and Shiner Blonde?"

"The truth? I didn't like it."

Letti looked horrified. "You didn't? I would have thought it would be everything you ever dreamed of."

"Guess again. The acting part was all right. I worked often enough. My agent got me a lot of small parts. A line or two here and there. Commercials. Low-budget stuff. Nothing that was going to set the world on fire or get me up out of the crowd. The rest of it didn't do much for me."

"But—but California is wonderful," she protested. "The weather, the beaches, the vibe. You didn't like any of that?"

"I had no time to enjoy the beach, between cattle calls and waiting tables in a third-rate restaurant to earn enough to pay LA rent. The traffic sucks and there's too damn many people. Too many wannabe stars vying for too few roles. I'm not saying I hated it, but I was thinking about coming home anyway when Renee was killed and Ross started falling off the deep end. Emma's as much as lost both her parents and Mom and Dad and I are trying to pick up the slack."

"Color me surprised. I thought your coming home was a big sacrifice."

"Like the one you made? Hardly."

"So what's next?"

"Law school. I'm starting St. Mary's in the fall. It's where Dad and Granddad got their law degrees."

"Them and almost every other lawyer in town." She paused a moment. "So how's Emma doing?"

"Okay, I guess." He leaned forward. "That's why she needs to play Ariel and I suspect that's why Jessica gave it to her. I don't know if she's going to be all that wonderful and I don't really care. For her, it's all about the healing."

"I know it's why Jessica gave it to her. She came out and said so." She made a face. "That was a fun conversation."

"Did you and Jessica ever come to a meeting of the minds?"

"No, and we're not going to. I understand why she gave the part to Emma and, believe it or not, I hope doing Ariel helps her heal. But I'm coming from a different place. I'm all about two things at the Durango. One is quality productions that will impress the Navarros and keep the big bucks coming our way, some of which is used to pay the employees, yourself included. The other is Sophie. That role would have been the exclamation point on the résumé we're sending to all the strong acting and theater programs around the country. That role was the last chance for her to do something big before the applications go out."

"And that's a big deal because…" he prompted.

"Because Sophie's going to have the chance I didn't. She's going to get her crack at a career in entertainment. Maybe I couldn't have it, but I'm going to make damned sure my daughter does." Her face lit up. "Sophie's got so much talent. More than I have, that's for sure. We've known it since she was five years old when she started singing and dancing and acting at the Durango. Now it's time to take it a step further. We're looking at schools on the east coast and California. I've taken her to the east coast and to the west, and she likes California better, so we'll probably concentrate on those schools. But the competition is fierce and she needs every advantage."

"Isn't her résumé already substantial? All I've heard since I went to work at the theater is Sophie this and Sophie that. I doubt one production's going to make a big difference."

"I hope you're right. And speaking of Sophie, colleges, and her résumé, I need to get back home and make sure she's downloaded the applications I told her to."

The waitress brought the check. He reached for his wallet but she beat him to it. "I can get that," he protested.

"Today's my treat. You can get it next time."

Excellent. She was planning on them having a next time. "In that case, thanks."

She paid and they walked out together. The hot sun shone down from the western sky. He looked up and over at her ruefully. "So much for a hot kiss to hold us until next weekend."

"Come with me." She took him by the hand and led him around the corner to a narrow grassy alley between the strip center and the beauty salon next door. "This private enough for you?"

"It'll do." He held out his arms and she stepped into them, wrapping her arms around his waist and pulling him close.

Her breath hitched in her throat as she stared up at him. "I'll be damned if I know why I want you so much. But I do," she whispered.

Their lips met, and she tasted of jalapeño and desire as he mapped her mouth. He didn't know what it was about her that excited him so. He couldn't explain it. All he knew was that she called to him like no other woman ever had.

She was the object of countless fantasies, and he was living one right now. Her fingers ran up his back, soft yet demanding. Even through their clothes, he could feel her nipples pebble. He fisted his hand in the lush, thick hair at her nape as they feasted on one another. His cock hardened, and she shivered in his arms.

He could tell she was as turned on as he was. A heady feeling to know that a passionate, beautiful woman like Letti desired him. He'd dreamed of her for the last five years, and he hoped she'd done the same.

Kevin was loath to let go of her, not sure how he was going to make it an entire week without her in his arms. "Are you sure those papers can't wait?" he asked breathlessly.

She nodded. "But one more until the weekend."

She framed his face between her hands. This kiss was different. Gentle and sweeter somehow, with all the passion of their first kiss, but none of the urgency. She raised her head. "Think that will hold us?"

Kevin ran his hands down her arms. "I guess it'll have to."

They walked back to their cars. "Until Friday," she said as she got in her crossover.

"Until Friday." He waited for her to back out before getting in the Mustang. He lowered the top and let the wind tease his hair as he headed out.

His lips tingled and his hard-on throbbed between his legs. He had a weekend with the sexiest woman in San Antonio, maybe the whole state of Texas. He was hot for her and she was just as hot for him.

Damn, he was glad he'd come home.

Life was good.

Friday couldn't come soon enough.

Chapter Eight

Letti threw on her black jeans and tee and ran a wide-toothed comb through her wet hair. She did the quickest makeup job on record and strapped on a pair of sandals. So much for taking pains with her appearance this afternoon. She'd gotten stuck in a ridiculously long conference with the fine arts dean and then sat cooling her heels on the expressway while they cleared a wreck blocking two out of three lanes.

Sophie and Marco were due at Owen's in twenty minutes and neither of them had packed a duffel. Her own bag for the weekend was already stashed in the crossover, filled with clothes that were mostly casual but with one slightly dressier pair of jeans and a sexy knitted top that showed off her curves. Kevin had been infuriatingly vague when she asked him what she needed. All he'd said for certain was to bring a swimsuit, which told her less than nothing. They could be doing anything from camping in a state park to living the high life in a Hill Country resort. He'd insisted on making the arrangements himself, which was a change. Owen had been good about going places and doing things, but the planning was all her responsibility.

It was nice to have the arrangements taken care of. And it would be interesting to see what Kevin came up with.

She was so ready for the weekend.

Her makeup finished, she put on a watch and a simple pair of earrings and loped down the stairs. Sophie and Marco were already in the foyer, Sophie clutching a thick stack of papers. "The applications," she said as she thrust them toward Letti.

"Took you long enough. Why are you handing them to me?"

"You wanted them. I printed them out. That's why I wasn't packed when you got here."

Letti stifled a sigh. "Sophie, I wanted the printouts so you could look at them. Most of these schools don't use a common application form, and you're going to have to fill out a different one for each school. You need to familiarize yourself with each school's requirements."

"Oh. I thought you wanted to see them. I'll look at them later." She laid the applications on the table in the entry.

Letti gritted her teeth. "Be sure that you do. Now, do you have everything you need for the weekend? Clothes, shoes, electronics?" Sophie and Marco had keys to the house, but she didn't want them coming by and discovering her AWOL for the weekend.

Sophie nodded. Marco patted his pocket and ran upstairs for his phone. "Tell your dad and Wade hello for me," she called after them as they headed for Sophie's car.

She took a minute she really didn't have and flipped through the applications. Damn, some of them were long. Thankfully Sophie could do them online, unlike the lengthy hand-written applications she'd had to send out. Unlike Letti, Sophie could count on her mother for help.

Letti took another minute to look at the applications and then put them in the desk drawer. She and Sophie had a lot of work ahead of them in the months to come.

She was halfway to the theater when the phone rang. She saw her mother's number and almost let it go to voice mail, but she didn't want her mother calling her later. She punched the button on the steering wheel. "Hello, Mom. What do you need? I'm on my way to the theater."

Her mother hesitated. "I know you said no more blind dates, but I was talking to Gloria Menchaca this morning and her brother is out of the service, and is going to be home in a couple of weeks. We thought maybe you'd like to meet him."

"I wouldn't. No more blind dates. Period. End of statement."

"But he sounds perfect," Mom wheedled. "He's only forty-two. He's divorced and has children so that's not an issue. She says he's very nice."

Letti sighed loudly so her mother would hear. "What do I have to do to get it through yours and *Abuela*'s heads that I'm not interested in any more of your blind dates? How many losers are you going to try to fix me up with before you get the message?"

"How do you know he's a loser?"

"How do you know he isn't?"

"Come on, Letti. Give the man a chance."

Letti's patience snapped. "Mom, I've had it. Quit pimping me out to your friends' unattached relatives. I. Am. Not. Interested."

She could hear her mother's gasp. "That-that's not what I'm trying to do."

"That's what it feels like. It's demeaning."

There was a moment of silence. "I-I'm sorry, *mija*. I only want you to be happy."

"I am happy," Letti said gently.

"All right. Are you coming over this weekend? Or do you have too much to do?"

Letti's lips twitched. *You could say that.* "It's finals at school and grading time," she reminded her mother. Not lying outright but not admitting she'd already turned in grades. "I'll see you next weekend."

Her mother wished her a good evening and ended the call. Letti punched the end button on her steering wheel. She shouldn't have snapped at her mother. But she was so damned tired of the campaign to find Letti a man and a happy ever after. She wasn't particularly interested in a happy ever after. Especially since her happy for now was spiriting her away for a weekend of sex, and whatever she needed her swimsuit for. She was so ready it wasn't funny.

Kevin was at the concession stand when she arrived at the Durango. Josh and Rachel were manning the will-call tickets and the lobby was filling with the friends and family of the high school cast. The Academy had so many teenaged students that Jessica had split them into two casts and crews.

Sophie's cast had performed last night. As usual, Sophie had knocked it out of the ballpark. Letti had gotten the teenage crew started last night and joined her mother and grandmother in their usual seats in the third row to cheer her daughter on. Tonight, she would escape to the balcony, where she would watch from the front row. A shiver ran down her back. Now that Kevin knew where her hideout was, maybe he would join her for a few minutes during the show. Maybe they would steal another kiss in the cubby behind the sound booth.

It would be a lovely start for the upcoming weekend.

She checked on things backstage, but the teenage crew had everything under control. She wandered back downstairs where she found Josh and Rachel talking to Jessica and Kevin. They all broke into big smiles for her. If Jessica bore a grudge, she wasn't letting it show. "Rachel sent out an email with the date of the next auditions," Josh said.

"What are you casting?" Kevin asked. "Anything I could play?"

"We're casting *South Pacific*," Rachel said. "There are roles in that one that would fit you to a T."

South Pacific. Kevin would be a wonderful Joseph Cable.

And Letti knew she'd be a perfect Nellie Forbush.

She wouldn't exactly be playing opposite him, but it would be fun to be in the same production. Especially if this weekend turned into something more than a one-time thing. The thought of which sent a chill down her back and had her body singing.

Kevin shot her a look that held all sorts of promise. He was thinking the same thing. He had to be.

She bought a soda and slipped upstairs to her spot in the front row, casting a critical eye as the performance proceeded. This cast, except for Laurey, was every bit as good as last night. But tonight it was difficult to get lost in the story when every fiber in her body quivered in anticipation of the weekend.

About two-thirds of the way through the first act, she sensed rather than heard Kevin come down the steps and ease quietly into the seat beside her. Almost absently he slipped his arm around her shoulders, the light touch of his fingers sending shivers from her head to her toes. She told herself she was being ridiculous. Too experienced to react like this to the mere touch of his hand.

Or maybe not.

What a lovely thought.

He stayed almost until intermission, leaving Letti practically squirming with thoughts of the night to come. His smile was genial behind the concession stand as he sold popcorn and sodas, but Letti could detect the slightest bit of tension in his jaw and an anticipatory gleam in his eyes. He was looking forward to the weekend as much as she was. It sent another shiver down her back. The thought that a man Kevin's age desired her the way he did confirmed she was nowhere near past it.

The second act seemed to go on forever. The curtain finally came down and Letti practically sprinted down the stairs. The teenaged crew had things well in hand and were ready to go home in less than ten minutes. Kevin was already standing beside his car when she left the theater. She looked at her car in dismay. She hadn't thought about the logistics. "How do you want to do this?" she asked. "Should we take both cars?"

"However you'd like. It would be kind of fun to do it together in the convertible."

She made a split-second decision. "Follow me to my place and we'll ditch mine."

It would look like she was home for the weekend if anybody wondered.

He entered her address in his GPS and pulled up in front of her house a minute after she did. They tossed her duffel in his trunk and he lowered the top. "Do you need a scarf?" he asked as he started the engine.

"Hell, no." She ran her fingers through her hair. "I'm good."

The wind whipped around her head, the night air balmy. They headed north, and down the state highway leading into the Hill Country. At Kevin's request, Letti kept her eyes peeled for the white-tailed deer who populated the cedar and oak-studded fields and pastures and darted out onto the highways.

They drove for the better part of an hour before Kevin turned onto the highway that would take them to the northern shore of Canyon Lake. Which explained the swimsuit.

"Mom and Dad have a condo on the water. I told them I was bringing friends up for the weekend. They're busy and aren't coming until Monday or Tuesday." He looked a little sheepish. "I hope that's all right. I'm pretty broke right now and can't do one of those fancy resorts."

"That's fine," she assured him. Actually, it made her feel like a teenager. It'd been years since she'd gone out with anyone young enough to be broke.

Letti kept her eyes peeled for deer as they headed toward the condo. They rounded a curve and she sucked in her breath as the lake came into view, moonlight dappling the water as gentle waves rippled the surface. He turned onto a two-lane road and they drove past a couple of subdivisions before he headed into a tony neighborhood close to the water. "Not exactly wilderness out here," she observed.

"Not like Lake Templeton where Wade grew up. He said Templeton has cattle drinking out of it in places."

"It's got some areas that are civilized. Sophie said he and Owen are planning a wedding on the beach in the little neighborhood in Verde. They aren't sure how many of the neighbors will show, but the whole community's invited."

Kevin glanced over at her. "Does it bother you?"

"It still pisses me off that Owen cheated. But I don't begrudge him his happiness. Everybody's entitled to that."

"Good for you."

"It took me awhile to get there," she admitted. This weekend was helping a lot, but she didn't need to tell Kevin that.

He rounded a corner and pulled up in front of a two-story waterfront building that appeared to be a four-plex. "It's not real big, but Mom and Dad bought it mostly for the boat dock that came with it. And the mini-beach the association maintains."

"A mini-beach. Hmm. Never heard of one of those before."

"That's why I asked you to bring the swimsuit." He grinned at her wickedly. "I hope there isn't much to it."

"Such an imagination," she laughed. She would surprise him tomorrow with the sexy number she'd brought.

The trunk held their duffels as well as a couple of grocery bags. He handed her the grocery bags and picked up the heavier duffels. "We can go out some and eat in some."

"Works for me."

They climbed the outside stairs and Kevin unlocked the door. "After you, milady."

Letti stepped inside and looked around. "Oh, how lovely."

Though not particularly large, the living room was warm and homey with dark blue leather furniture that looked elegant and comfortable. One wall had a wide-screen TV and bookshelves stuffed with what looked like a wide variety of paperbacks. The wall facing the lake had floor-to-ceiling windows with a sliding glass door on one end leading to a balcony. A galley kitchen and big dining alcove sat off to one side. The other side had a hall, probably leading to bedrooms. The unit lacked the musty smell of disuse, leading her to believe someone was here often. "Did you grow up coming here?"

"Sure did. They bought it when I was four, maybe. Along with the boat out there, we've gotten a lot of use out of it over the years. Before things went south, Ross and Renee would bring Emma. Now that Dad's semi-retired, he and Mom like to spend some of their weekdays here so they can do the social scene on the weekends. Is it all right?"

"Quit angst-ing. It's lovely." She carried the grocery bags to the kitchen, and together they unloaded the food, brushing up against each other in the narrow kitchen. With each touch she became more aware of him. His woodsy shampoo, aftershave, and his essence. His square jaw and kissable lips. His muscular arms and shoulders. His perfect butt encased in tight jeans. His dancing blue eyes, burning with desire *for her*.

She could hardly wait for what she knew was coming.

He put away the last of the perishables, and stared at one another for a moment. *This is it.* The moment they had been moving toward since she'd barged into Jessica's office. It had been inevitable that they would end up back in one another's arms. The need was too strong, the desire too great. Nothing would ever come of it, she knew that and so did he, but for now it was right. It was where they needed to be tonight.

The future could take care of itself.

They moved together as one, their lips meeting as he enfolded her into his arms. Sweet, so sweet, his lips on hers, his arms holding her. Longing flooded her body, responding to the strength of his. Desire surged as they clung together for long moments.

Now that she was in his arms, she was in no particular hurry to take things to the next level. They would get there, and she would savor every sweet moment of the journey. They had all night…all weekend.

They kissed and caressed. Her nipples hardened and the vee between her legs grew damp. He raised his head and said, "I know where there's a king-sized bed with our names on it. Wanna try it out?"

"Naw, kitchen floor's fine."

Kevin shook his head. "Ever the snark."

Before she could stop him he whisked her off her feet into his arms and strode through the condo, taking her into a small but gorgeous room dominated by a king-sized bed. The only other furniture was an old-fashioned dresser and a boudoir chair. An entire wall of floor-to-ceiling windows faced the lake. The drapes were open and moonlight sparkled on the water, illuminating the room with a silvery sheen. Kevin lowered Letti on the bed and lay down beside her.

"I finally have you where I want you," he teased. His face sobered. "I've dreamed of this. Five years I've dreamed of having you back in my arms. You ruined me. For. Every. Other. Woman."

"And I'll bet you spent plenty of time making sure of that," she jibed.

His eyes danced. "I did. But seriously, none of them held a candle to you." He covered her, pressing her into the comforter as he covered her face with kisses.

She ran her hands down his arms. Now that she was here, she could admit that she too had dreamed of their night together, having wild, out-of-control sex in a San Antonio hotel room.

Now, they were about to do it again.

Kevin sat up and in a single motion pulled off his shirt. "Too many clothes for what comes next." He kicked off his tennis shoes and shucked his pants and briefs, leaving him naked in the darkened room.

In the silvery bright moonlight shining off the water, she saw he'd changed in the intervening years. His shoulders were broader than she remembered. His chest was wider and the peach fuzz had grown into a generous sprinkling of light brown hair. His waist and hips were more muscular.

But his cock remained unchanged: long and thick and ready for her.

She looked down at her still-clothed body with sudden apprehension. She'd seen changes in his body. He was bound to see changes in hers. But where his changes were for the better, hers certainly were not. She was five years older, five years less firm, five years less supple than she had been. She hesitated for a moment. Fuck it. He'd sought her out, pressed for this. He knew she wasn't in her twenties.

In a movement mirroring Kevin's, she pulled the black tee over her head. Her sandals went flying and her jeans hit the floor, leaving her clad in a lacy demi bra and matching panties.

Kevin put his hands on her waist and turned her to face him. "Now, that's a pretty picture." He tongued one of her nipples through the lace. "But that's still more clothes than I had in mind."

With deft fingers that spoke of practice, he undid the bra and whipped the lacy confection from her body. Her lacy panties were next, leaving her naked to his eyes. He sucked in his breath. "Even more beautiful than I remember." He reached out and almost reverently touched the tip of her breast with his finger. "It's fuller than it was. Lusher. You've gotten prettier, Letti. More beautiful than ever."

She started to demur, but stopped herself. If he thought she was more beautiful, she wasn't going to argue with him. Instead she ran her hand down the middle of his chest to his washboard abs.

"You got better, too." She let her hand drift lower, tangling in the flare of soft brown hair surrounding his erect cock before encasing it in her hand.

He reached down and gently removed her fingers. "You need to stop that or this is going to be over before we've started."

"Then let's get a move on."

They lay facing each other. Despite his youth, he seemed in no hurry to get down to it. He took his time, starting with a deep, soulful kiss and then kissing his way down her body, nibbling on her neck and sending shock waves through her when he latched onto her breast, teasing it into a hard peak. He gave her other breast the same attention, murmuring words of admiration as he feasted on them.

His praise was as much as turn-on as his touch, and Letti reveled in the knowledge that he found her beautiful and desirable. His lips drifted lower, to her waist and below. "Sexy," he murmured as he rubbed his cheek against her stomach. "Like Marilyn Monroe."

"You a fan of Marilyn Monroe?"

"Oh, yeah. And Raquel Welch. Grew up jacking off to *One Million Years BC* and *Some Like it Hot*." His smile was wolfish. "I know what's sexy and what's not. And you, lady, are definitely sexy."

She was good with that.

He continued kissing his way down her stomach to her well-groomed curls. "Open up," he said, swatting her thigh lightly. "I'm about to feast."

Her heart started to pound. She loved it when a man wanted to go down on her.

She parted her legs and he angled himself between them. His breath was warm as he parted her folds with his fingers. "You're so pretty and so ready. I love that you're hot like this *for me.*"

The touch of his tongue had her almost coming off the bed. He had learned a few things from those California women. Five years ago, he'd been willing but inexperienced. This man knew his way around a woman's body.

He had her gasping and writhing as his tongue expertly drew her to a pulsing high that had her tumbling over the edge quickly, tremors tearing through her body in the most intense orgasm she'd ever experienced in her life. It had been a while, and this man was skilled.

She gasped out his name over and over, the aftershocks almost as hard as the orgasm itself. She felt herself sinking down into the bed. "Damn. That was…that was…I don't have a word for what that was."

"Good?" he suggested helpfully.

"That's like saying the Mona Lisa's a nice picture."

"Well, it is." He peeked up from between her legs. "How many more do you want to go for?"

"Are you kidding? You think I can do that again?"

"You better believe it."

"Prove me wrong."

"My pleasure."

He bent his head and, clearly enjoying himself, he had her screaming again. He barely let her catch her breath before his lips began to work their magic for a third time, bringing her to yet another earth-shattering climax.

"Told you." He looked smug as he sat up. He scowled, then said, "Hell, they're in the other room. You'd think I would be savvier than that."

"Than what?"

"Than leaving the duffel with the condoms in the living room. Be right back." He hopped out of bed, unmindful of his nudity or the huge hard-on he was sporting.

Letti's lips twitched. This was one of the ways he reminded her he was still twenty-five years old. The condom wasn't necessary on her part. She hadn't had a period in couple of months and hadn't had sex since the last time she'd been tested. But she had no idea about Kevin's recent sexual history, and wasn't going to take any chances.

He reappeared a moment later clutching a handful of condoms.

"Optimistic much?" she teased.

"Realistic." He ripped open a package and had the condom on before she could volunteer to help. He dipped down and took her mouth in a deep, wet, long kiss. Then settled between her legs, easing his length into her body. "Damn," he breathed as he buried himself to the hilt. "So fuckin' good."

He paused before beginning to move inside her. His motions were gentle at first, but his rhythm sped up, and his arms slid under her back, his hands grasping her shoulders.

She'd thought herself spent, and had been wrong. He kept hitting that spot deep inside her, thrusting faster, and she began to spiral, crying out as yet another orgasm shook her body.

He thrust twice more before his own powerful orgasm overtook him with a shout as his cock pulsed within her. They clung together, him breathing hard into her neck, her shuddering with aftershocks.

After his breathing leveled out, they rolled to their sides, not breaking contact. He touched her forehead with his. "You're a phenomenal fuck," he murmured. "Better than I remember."

"Not so bad yourself." Her body was a boneless mass of satisfied.

"Better than five years ago?"

"Much better. Why?"

He looked at her and grinned. "I hoped this time you didn't think I needed tutoring."

She laughed. "You only needed a few pointers then, and you sure don't need any now."

Her stomach rumbled and she looked down ruefully. "Sorry. I left the house late and didn't have dinner."

"What I had wore off awhile back." He eased out of her, and sat up. "After I get rid of this," he looked down at his half-hard cock, "let's grab a bite before we go in for round two. And three. And four."

"Ah, the pleasures of youth."

He shook his head. "You know better than that. Women don't reach their sexual peak until they're well into their thirties. We guys, on the other hand, hit thirty and it's all downhill from there. Which would make us perfectly matched, wouldn't it?"

She reached out and wound her arms around his neck. "Yeah, perfectly matched."

Chapter Nine

Letti smiled and turned over on her beach towel. The late morning sun beat down on her back and her thighs. It was probably time for another application of sunscreen, but she hated the stuff and would rather chance a bit of a burn than have to spray on more the greasy stuff. She glanced over at Kevin. He definitely needed more. He was tan for an Anglo, but still several shades lighter than her natural brown. Unlike some Hispanic women, she didn't mind getting darker in the sun, and by the middle of June would have a rich, healthy glow. If he came up here every so often, he'd have a rich tan in a few weeks.

Maybe they could come up here again and get those tans together.

She crossed her arms in front of her and laid her head on them. She ached in places she hadn't ached in a long time. Places that had gotten a real workout this weekend. She wouldn't mind going another round or two before they got back in his convertible and went home later this afternoon. She glanced over at him. Most likely, he'd be up for it.

He had been up for most of the weekend.

Which was wonderful. It had been exactly what she needed.

They'd made fat sandwiches and eaten them cross-legged and naked in bed before another round of scorching sex. Kevin woke up Saturday morning hard and eager, leading to some interesting gymnastics in the large shower. She made him *migas* for breakfast while he packed a picnic lunch.

He gassed up the boat and they'd spent a good part of the day motoring around the large, winding lake, exploring the alcoves and waving to the boaters and skiers sharing the waves with them.

While the heavily populated lake was much too public for sex in the boat, they did manage a steamy kiss every so often, which had them both primed for more incredible sex.

She'd modeled the enticing swimsuit, with its daring cut-outs and barely there mesh connecting the top to the bottom. Later, they went to the nearby grocery and got a couple of rib-eyes to grill for dinner. They'd sat together on a beach towel and watched the sun go down and the stars come out. By the time they'd come inside and showered off the sand, it was time to burn off all that food.

Her body responded like it never had before, and was an affirmation she was still a desirable woman. It'd been balm to her ego that they'd spent most of the weekend busy in bed.

She yawned and looked at her watch. "Damn. It's almost noon. I thought we had more time."

Kevin shrugged. "We do." He looked at her curiously. "Why do you wear that?"

"Wear what?"

"A watch. You have the time on your phone."

"Force of habit, I guess."

He sat up. "I never got in the habit."

"You and every person younger than me," she said. "I've never seen Josh or Rachel wear one. Owen wears an Apple watch, and I think he bought Wade one. I wonder if they're going to audition for *South Pacific* since they're planning a wedding."

"Two dudes planning a wedding. I'd like to be a fly on the wall for that one."

She grinned. "Wade's mother's taking care of it for them. Neither of them have the decorator/event-planner gene. If they don't audition that leaves it wide open, and there's some good roles in it for guys. You'd be an awesome Joseph Cable."

"I don't know. Singing isn't my strong point."

"It's not your weak point either. You're a tenor, right? I heard you sing during *White Christmas*. You did fine."

"Thanks."

"It would be fun," she went on. "You could do Joseph Cable. And if I get cast as Nellie Forbush, we wouldn't exactly be cast opposite one another but we'd still have some numbers together."

Kevin hesitated before he asked, "Why would you want to play Nellie Forbush?"

"Why wouldn't I? She's the lead and the heroine of the whole story. It's mezzo soprano. The range is perfect for me. And I can do whatever they choreograph. I've always wanted to play Nellie." Her eyes narrowed. "Unless you think the role should go to a white girl. A blonde."

"Please. That's insulting," he said. "Nellie Forbush is supposed to be in her mid-twenties. I think the biography says she's twenty-four. They're not going to cast you as Nellie, even if you're the best singer and dancer they have."

Letti felt her face turn red. "Well, shit. You saying I'm too *old* to play Nellie?"

"That's exactly what I'm saying. That part will go to a girl in her twenties. I have no doubt you could knock it out of the ballpark. But you won't get the part."

"Jesus. Why don't you tell me what you really think?" She stood up and jerked her towel up off the beach.

He thought she couldn't play a woman in her twenties. He thought she was too old to play Nellie.

He thought she was old, period.

The little fucker.

Kevin jumped up and jerked up his towel. "I didn't say you were old. I said you're too old to play Nellie, because you are. Why don't you audition for Bloody Mary?"

"*Bloody Mary?* That's an old woman's role. She's Liat's mother."

"So? You're Sophie's mother. Liat's supposed to be about Sophie's age."

"Because I don't want to play Liat's mother. I don't want to play Sophie's mother. I don't want to play *anybody's* mother. And I sure as hell don't want to play an old woman. No actor in their right mind plays older."

She shook her towel, not caring that most of the loose sand fell on him, and marched toward the condo, Kevin on her heels.

"Letti, you're being ridiculous. A lot of actors and actresses play older. Marlon Brando in *The Godfather*. Elizabeth Taylor in *Giant* and again in *Who's Afraid of Virginia Woolf?*. Geena Davis in *A League of Their Own*. Angela Lansbury in *Manchurian Candidate*. It's the sign of a serious actor. Are you serious or aren't you?"

"Really? I'm plenty serious." She stomped up the stairs and threw open the sliding door. "It's a matter of not wanting to be old. If I play a part like that, I may as well put a sticker that says 'old lady' on my forehead. You may think I'm old. But I'm not."

"Shit. Don't twist my words. Use your head." Kevin stomped up the stairs and leaned into her. "Do you think I would've fucked your brains out all weekend if I thought you were old? Do you think I'd be hard as steel right now if I thought you were old?"

Letti whirled around and stomped into the condo, Kevin right behind her, and found herself staring into the stunned faces of Byron and Barbara Summerset.

***

Well, shit.

What a moment for his parents to show up.

He and Letti may as well have been going at it on the sofa.

His mom and dad were standing in the living room with shock on their faces and small suitcases at their feet. Letti froze in her tracks, nearly falling to her knees when he smacked into her. He grabbed her by her shoulders to steady her.

"Fuck," he breathed into her ear.

From the looks on their faces, his parents heard every word he and Letti had hurled at one another. He felt the blood rush to his face as he looked at them in horror. If there had been a crack in the floor wide enough, he would have gladly fallen through it.

The Summersets looked from him to Letti and back to him. He made sure she was steady on her feet before stepping beside her. "Mom, Dad. I didn't know you were coming this early."

"Obviously not," his father said dryly.

His mother looked distressed. "W-we t-thought you w-were c-coming w-with a c-college f-friend. W-we d-didn't realize…" His mother trailed off helplessly, her stammer worse than usual. No doubt aided by having heard her twenty-five-year-old son had spent the weekend 'fucking the brains out' of his forty-year-old lover.

They all four stared at one another for a long, uncomfortable moment, His parents eyed Letti's *Sports Illustrated* swimsuit, and his bare chest and board shorts.

His mind raced, but he had no idea what to say or do. Letti used her gracious voice and said, "It's good to see you this morning. Your condo is lovely. I so enjoyed coming here. Do you get to use it often?"

Okay. Letti was going to use social graces to smooth things over. His mother immediately picked up on what Letti was trying to do. "Y-yes, we're h-here a l-lot during the week. B-Byron and I b-both l-like to f-fish. D-did y-you and K-Kevin g-go f-fishing?"

"No, we didn't. But Kevin took me out in your boat. We had a lovely time on the water."

Kevin and his father stood silently while Letti and his mother traded a few more pleasantries. Then Letti turned to Kevin. "Now that your mom and dad are here, we need to head back to town." She turned to his parents. "Give us a few minutes and we'll be out of your hair." She exited as if they were fully clothed and were holding martinis, her head held high and completely composed.

Now what? His mother stared at him in dismay. His father looked him up and down and bit his lip. His expression was stern but his eyes were twinkling.

Damn. His old man was trying not to laugh.

Time to get moving. "Let me get this sand off me and my clothes changed so I can take Letti home."

"No need to hurry," his father said. "Get changed and your stuff packed and your mother and I will treat you and Letti to lunch."

He groaned inwardly. It might be all right. Or he and Letti might be subjected to an interrogation. Subtle, but an interrogation nevertheless. His first inclination was to refuse. But under the circumstances, that really wasn't an option.

Letti was running a comb through her wet hair when he joined her in the bathroom. She had showered and was dressed in black jeans with gold stars trailing down one leg, and a classy-looking knit blouse that showed off her curves.

"I'm sorry. I never thought they'd come up early."

"It is what it is," she said tersely. "It could have been a lot worse. Your parents have too much breeding to make a scene." She pointed to the shower. "I'll get the sheets off the bed while you clean up. We can be out of their hair in less than ten." She glanced into the bedroom. "God. I bet this is their bedroom. How embarrassing."

Kevin kicked out of his swimsuit. "We're not the first to use their room and we won't be the last. As far as getting out of their hair, they invited us out for lunch before we go."

"They *what?*"

"They asked us out to lunch. Under the circumstances, I wasn't about to turn them down."

"Either your mom and dad have cornered the market on civility, or we're about to get the third degree."

"Ya think?"

"So where are some fresh sheets?"

"Fresh sheets? Why?"

"Are you kidding? Because those smell like *we fucked our brains out all weekend.*"

Thank god women thought of things like that.

Letti put on makeup and made quick work of changing the sheets while he showered. They shoved their dirty clothes in the duffels, both of them went down on their hands and knees to check under everything to make sure all their underwear was collected off the floor.

When they were sure the room was as they found it, Letti sighed, he shrugged, then he picked up their bags and they went into the living room where his parents appeared to have recovered from their shock and were unloading their groceries into the refrigerator.

His dad suggested an upscale restaurant overlooking the water. Kevin tossed his and Letti's bags in the trunk, and they got in his car and followed his father's Lexus to the restaurant.

"I've heard of this place but I've never been here," she murmured as they pulled in beside the Lexus.

"They don't come here often. Consider yourself honored."

"Or they're softening us up for the grilling."

"That too."

The hostess escorted them to a table next to the window overlooking the water. He was nervous. Not for his own sake, but for Letti's. But to their credit, his parents were absolutely lovely. Conversation for the most part stayed general, revolving mostly around the theater, past and upcoming productions.

The only real questioning from his parents was regarding Sophie and her college plans, which Letti was more than happy to expound upon. He knew damn well his mother was dying to know what was going on and would probably ask about it later. But his mom and his dad had taken the high road, and silently he thanked them for it.

They feasted on catfish and shrimp with all the sides. Letti excused herself to go to the restroom and his mother spotted friends across the room and went to say hello. Their server brought the check and his father paid.

Dad leaned back and crossed his arms in front of him. "You and Letti Aldrete, huh? Didn't see that coming."

His father didn't know about their one-night stand five years ago. Kevin never said anything, and left shortly after. Letti surely never said anything.

"Yeah, me and Letti. She's a great person." He hated the defensiveness in his voice.

"Yes, she is. And a sexy one too. Every straight man at that theater lusts after her. I don't know what that fool she was married to was thinking, leaving her for a man. Hell, if it weren't for your mother—" His father smirked.

"Not a mental image I was looking for, Dad."

"Neither's the mental image you and your lover presented your mother and me with this morning. Fucking her brains out. That's a good one."

"Sorry about that."

Dad snickered. "Kevin, I'm not passing judgment. She's one hell of a woman, and if she's up for a good time with you, have fun. But that's my point. Have your fling. But you both need to remember that a fling is all it is. Short and sweet, with a definite expiration date. You don't have any business committing to something long-term with a woman her age."

Kevin wasn't surprised by the sudden spurt of indignation, which quickly turned to embarrassment for Letti when he turned around and spotted her a couple of tables away.

From the look on her face he knew she'd heard every word his father said. Although she quickly schooled her expression, he could tell his father's comments stung.

His mother rejoined them and they left the restaurant a few minutes later. He waited until they were on the highway to speak. "I'm sorry Dad said what he did. You didn't deserve that."

Letti made a face and shook her head. "He's like every other man out there. All for Junior having a good time. If it's with a sexy cougar, have at it. I don't know whether to be flattered that he thinks I'm hot or pissed that he doesn't want you to get serious with a woman 'my age.'" She made air quotes with her fingers.

"It was the age part that got to you."

"If he'd left my birthdays out of it, I wouldn't have thought a thing of his comments. He's right. You and me, we're a fun fling with an expiration date. Which has probably come and gone, if your mother has anything to say about it."

"Which she doesn't," he snapped. Whoa, where did that come from? He was feeling things for Letti he hadn't expected to. "Mom doesn't have a thing to say about it," he said more gently. "Nor does my father. Letti, this weekend was magic. Pure magic. I felt it and I know you did as well."

"I did." She reached over and put her hand on his thigh. The touch of her fingers made him start to get hard. Again.

He gestured to his cock. "That's what I mean. You barely touched me and I'm off like a rocket. I want more of that. I'm not ready to call it quits after one weekend."

"I'm not either. I'd like to continue the magic, at least for a little while."

"Then let's go for it. When can I see you again?"

Chapter Ten

Word had gotten out about her and Kevin.

She stared down at her phone in consternation. At least twenty texts had come in during the day from her theater friends. Four had sent thumbs up. The rest ranged from: "WTF?" "Good going." "RAWR." "Go, mama." Hearts. And one "How'd you manage that? Details!"

She'd known it was coming. Tandy Watson was one of the sweetest Academy moms around, but also had one of the biggest mouths. It was inevitable that she would share the news that she'd run into them having breakfast together at a coffee shop. From the volume of texts, Tandy must have announced it from the stage using a bullhorn.

At least her theater friends were supportive, even if they were amused. Not everyone was going to be. Letti groaned at the sound of her mother's ringtone. She clicked on her phone. "Whatcha need, Mom? I'm on my way to the theater."

"What's this I hear from Sophie about you and this young boy at the theater? She called me last night practically in tears about her mother and this...this *muchacho*. What are you thinking, Letti?"

"I'm thinking that I'm feeling good about myself for the first time in five years. I'm thinking it's time for me to do something besides work and be a mother. I'm thinking it's none of anybody's business. I'm also thinking it's time my daughter quit running to her *abuela* with her complaints and take them up with me directly."

"She has a right to complain. She's embarrassed."

"I don't know why. It's not like I'm kissing Kevin in the lobby of the Durango. We've kept it private."

"So how did she find out?"

"One of the Academy moms ran into us eating breakfast together one morning. I have no doubt the woman spread the word. Look, you told me to get out there and date. That's what I'm doing. I'm seeing a good guy, and having the time of my life."

"You're making a fool of yourself," her mother hissed. "He's only in it to get you to pay for things."

Letti laughed out loud. "Sure. Byron and Barbara Summerset's son needs Letti Aldrete to pay his way to the damn movies."

Her mother was quiet for a minute. "You're dating the son of those rich people? *Hijole*, what are they gonna think?"

"I don't know what they think. But they were a hell of a lot nicer about it than you're being."

"They *know?*"

"They do, and they don't seem to mind. So maybe you could try a little of the same."

"What about Sophie? She's horrified. And so is your *abuela*."

"If she's okay with her father marrying a young hottie, she can cut me the same slack and be okay with me dating a young hottie. If she says one damned word to me, I will tell her so in words of one syllable. And there's no way I'm going to please *Abuela* anyway, so why even try?"

"You're making a fool of yourself. Even if he is paying."

"Maybe. But I'm happier than I've been since Owen walked out the door. I'm having fun in the here and now. It's too bad you can't be a little happy for me." She clicked off her phone before her mother had a chance to answer.

Letti threw the phone down on the bed and swapped out her *chanklas* for shoes she could dance in if she had to. The yoga pants and tee she had changed into after teaching her class this morning would be fine for the audition.

Her mother's phone call pissed her off. No matter what she did, they would find something wrong with it. Not that she expected anything different. They wouldn't see the value in a relationship that wouldn't lead to something permanent. In their eyes, if a woman wasn't married, she didn't have a man's protection. Ugh.

Regardless of their beliefs, they could at least be nice about it, and she would make it clear that was what she expected.

She pushed that thought aside and pulled her hair into a short ponytail to get it off her neck. A little makeup and she was ready to go. She stuck her head into Marco's room, where he was playing a video game. He'd spent most of the morning on the soccer field and smelled like it. "Leftover casserole in the fridge. And for crying out loud, before your dad and Wade pick you up, *have a shower.*"

He mumbled something she took as assent. The brutal June heat beat down as she sprinted for the car, burning her hand on the door handle. Sophie was already at the theater, having spent the day at the Academy as a volunteer with the younger students. Letti had been thrilled when Jessica invited Sophie to intern at the Academy. Maybe it was a consolation prize for the role of Ariel going to Emma, but with a letter of recommendation from Jessica, it would look wonderful on Sophie's résumé. Letti hadn't gone to any of the Academy *Little Mermaid* rehearsals, but Sophie said Emma was doing a good job with the role.

The last two weeks of rehearsals for the adult cast had begun, and next week was dreaded tech week, otherwise known as dead week, when everything had to come together. Letti loved the electric excitement of that last week as the cast and crew put everything together for a show to be proud of. It was wonderful to experience as crew chief.

It was even more exciting as a cast member.

Letti pushed that thought aside. Tonight they were holding auditions for *South Pacific.* Maybe she would be cast this time. She would sing something generic, something the ensemble sang. That way, Rachel couldn't accuse her of gunning for Nellie Forbush. But if she happened to sing better than any of the other women trying out, they would have to give Nellie to her.

The parking lot was full and the regulars were assembled in the auditorium. Letti wandered up to the lobby and helped herself to a soda, leaving money in the refrigerator. She detoured into the ladies' room and was about to head into the auditorium when Owen ran into the lobby, Wade on his heels. "What's this I hear about you and Kevin Summerset?" Owen demanded. "Everybody in the theater's talking about you."

Letti's eyes narrowed. "Exactly what did you hear and who did you hear it from?"

"Everybody."

"Nope. Names, Owen. I need names."

"Well, uh." He looked embarrassed. "One of the Academy mothers apparently saw you and the boy out together and told Jessica and everyone else who would listen. Jesus, Letti, what are you thinking? He's fifteen years younger than you. He's practically a boytoy. Aren't you embarrassed?"

She looked from him to Wade. "I don't know. Aren't you? I'm just screwing around with my boytoy. You're marrying yours."

Owen's mouth flew open and Wade started laughing. "She's got you there. They're fifteen years apart. We're fifteen years apart."

"Well, hell." Owen looked flummoxed. "But you're embarrassing Sophie."

"Who is standing right over there listening to this entire exchange," Wade said dryly.

Letti motioned to Sophie. "Come here, Soph. I have a few words to say to you. And I'm going to say them in front of your father so you both understand me completely."

Sophie's eyes widened and she crossed the lobby. "Now, not only has your grandmother jumped down my throat for embarrassing you, but your father also felt the need to weigh in. You, your father, and your grandmother all need to understand something. Who I choose to date is my business and mine alone. It is not yours, your father's, or your *abuela*'s. You had no business talking to anyone but me about how you feel about what I do with my life. Understood?"

Sophie nodded, looking none too happy. "Furthermore, if you're okay with your father marrying a man fifteen years his junior, you can be equally okay with me dating one. Or do I not deserve the same consideration he gets?"

"She's right, Sophie. It's none of our business," Owen said gently. "Your mom deserves our respect."

"Okay, Daddy. Sorry, Mom." She turned on her heel and went back to the Academy faster than a bullet.

"My. That went well," Letti snapped. "I deserve the same respect out of her she gives to you."

"And you'll get it," Owen said. "I'll make sure she understands."

"But you're her mom. And somehow moms are different." Wade shrugged.

"Speaking of moms, how's yours coming planning your wedding?" Letti asked. "And what are the two of you doing at auditions tonight? Shouldn't you be getting ready for the big day?"

"Mom's got it under control. So much so that we're going to go ahead and try out. We can handle a couple of the smaller parts and still do the wedding stuff."

"A smaller role?" she asked. "I'd have thought you'd be trying out for Joseph Cable."

"I don't know that I'd get it. Kevin's auditioning."

Good. A little chill ran down Letti's back. She and Kevin could be acting with one another. Nellie had several scenes with Joseph Cable.

That would be awesome.

They turned toward the auditorium when Josh and Rachel poked their heads in the lobby. Rachel caught Letti's eye and motioned her over. "Could we have a word with you?"

Letti nodded and Wade and Owen disappeared into the auditorium. They approached her looking a bit unsure of themselves. Her curiosity stirred, she nodded. "What's on your mind?"

Josh and Rachel looked at one another. "Spit it out," Rachel said to Josh.

Josh took a deep breath. "I know you want to play Nellie, but that's not happening. But we do desperately need you in the production. Your talent's being wasted as crew chief."

Letti's spirits sank. "It's not worth it to me to be in the ensemble," she stated. "I know it's a crappy attitude, but that's how I feel."

"No, no. Not ensemble." Josh looked at Rachel anxiously.

Rachel took a deep breath. "We want you to play Bloody Mary."

"*What*? You got to be kidding. Bloody Mary's an old woman."

"Not necessarily," Rachel said quickly. "She's old enough to have an almost grown daughter, which doesn't mean she's necessarily all that old." She raised her eyebrow and looked at Letti pointedly. "Lots of actresses who aren't all that old have played her."

"And there's another reason." Josh looked at her seriously. "Bloody Mary's a difficult sell in today's climate. The character's politically incorrect, and not every actress out there can push her past the cliché of a native woman speaking pidgin English who wants to make money off the sailors and finagle her daughter a rich husband. You could do it. You could make her human. You could bring to life the person beneath the stereotype. You could convey her deep desire for her daughter to have a better life. You could deliver the outrageous dialogue and make it work." He glanced around and lowered his voice. "To be honest, we have nobody else in there who could pull it off. *Please*, Letti. We need you."

"Nice butter up. She's still old," Letti protested.

"So we do a little aging makeup," Rachel said reasonably.

"And we cast your own daughter to play Liat."

Letti's next protest died on her lips. "You'd cast Sophie as Liat? You want me to play Bloody Mary that badly?"

"Yes," they said in unison.

"Sophie would do a marvelous job," Rachel added. "It would be a nice exclamation point for her college applications. Her first role in an adult production."

"Think about it. You and Sophie, playing mother and daughter," Josh coaxed.

"I don't know about this. What about auditions? Is a foregone conclusion fair to the others?"

Rachel looked at her disbelievingly. "Since when does that matter to you?"

Letti felt her face turn red. "I... well..."

"Everyone's audition will be considered, and if one of them blows us away, fine," Josh said. "But I don't expect it to happen." He paused a minute. "Tell you what. You come in and audition like you were going to do. Get Sophie in there, too. Listen for yourself and see if you can understand why we want you to do this."

Letti nodded, and Rachel and Josh went back in the auditorium.

She punched in Sophie's number. "Where are you?"

"I'm helping Jessica put stuff up and then I'm going home."

"Change of plans. Finish up with Jessica and come on over. Josh wants you to audition."

"Oh. Really? Ah, okay. I'll be over in a minute." Sophie hung up.

Letti put her phone back in her pocket. That was odd. Sophie didn't seem too excited. She would have thought her daughter would have been a lot more enthusiastic at a chance to perform in one of the adult productions.

Letti wandered into the auditorium. Now that the cat was out of the bag, she saw no reason why she and Kevin shouldn't sit together. She slid in beside him. "You decided to audition after all."

He grinned. "I find myself missing acting more than I thought I would. This could be a nice fix."

"Not over LA after all?" she teased.

"Plenty over it. Not over acting."

"You won't ever get over that."

She slipped her hand into his and looked around. She knew some of the people. The visibly pregnant Vivienne Abonce sat between her husband Miguel and her brother, board chairman Cameron Heiser. Their presence made her wonder. Cameron was probably here in his role as board chairman, but Miguel wasn't an actor and Vivienne was too close to delivery to be in the production.

Wade and Owen were a couple of rows behind them. Production manager Miranda Jenks sat off to one side, watching quietly. Letti's heart went out to the woman. There was no real reason for Miranda to be here tonight. But the lonely woman would rather be here than at her house on a small ranch outside Pleasanton, remembering her dead son and fighting the temptation to pour herself a drink.

There were people she didn't know. Young mostly, but a couple of older men who were probably interested in playing Emile de Becque or Captain Brackett.

As Rachel stepped to the mic, the auditorium door opened and a strikingly beautiful young woman with strawberry blonde hair slipped in and scurried down the aisle, sitting about halfway to the stage. Letti eyed the newcomer. She'd never seen the girl before, and from the curious looks the young woman was getting, nobody else had either.

Rachel went into her usual spiel and the rehearsal pianist took her place behind the keyboard. They began the audition process. The first five candidates took their place on the stage and each sang a number of their choice from *South Pacific* and delivered a few lines. Ensemble material for sure, and a couple had potential for later productions. As was the way at the Durango, all were praised and thanked and given words of encouragement.

The ensemble members of today were the leads of tomorrow.

Sophie was in the third group. Letti whipped her head around and breathed a sigh of relief when Sophie came down the aisle. Her daughter did her usual wonderful job and received an enthusiastic round of applause. Letti squirmed in her chair. If she played Bloody Mary, Sophie was a shoo-in for Liat. Sophie would be a wonderful Liat.

A thought crossed her mind. If she was cast as Bloody Mary and Kevin as Joseph Cable, most of her scenes in the play would be opposite Kevin. They would be playing opposite one another for most of the show.

Another thought crossed her mind and Letti froze. If Sophie was cast as Liat and Kevin as Joseph Cable, her daughter and her lover would have to pull off an onstage kiss. They would have a tender scene the morning after they had made love all night.

That thought did not make Letti happy.

Kevin was in the next set of hopefuls called to the stage. When it was his turn, he sang a poignant rendition of "Younger than Springtime" that sent chills down Letti's back. She didn't know what he meant about not having a singing voice. He sang beautifully and was treated to a round of applause at the end.

Letti's name was called in the next round. Her heart pounded in her throat as she climbed the stairs to the stage. They wanted her to play Bloody Mary. So that's what she would give them. She turned to a section of dialogue in the script and did her best to deliver a few lines in the character's broken English before nodding to the pianist and breaking into "Bali Ha'i," Bloody Mary's signature song. There was a moment of silence after the last reverberating note, and then the theater erupted in spontaneous applause. Josh was all smiles and Rachel gave her a big thumbs-up.

The role was hers if she wanted it.

But, did she want it?

Letti sighed and returned to her seat. She would be a fool not to take it. Especially since it would guarantee her daughter the role of Liat. It was a bribe, pure and simple. A bribe she would take for her daughter's sake.

Kevin's eyes danced as he leaned over. "I thought you didn't want to play Bloody Mary. What made you change your mind?"

"I'll tell you later," she whispered.

The rest of the auditions took the better part of another hour. Wade and Owen did their usual wonderful jobs and were sure to be cast. A darling brother and sister pair sang *Dites Moi* and would be delightful as Ngana and Jerome, the de Becque children.

To her surprise, Josh called Cameron's name and their board chairman delivered an incredible rendition of "Some Enchanted Evening." Apparently, Cameron had decided to make one of his rare appearances on the stage. Letti hoped he was cast. He spent entirely too much time behind the scenes and nowhere nearly enough in front of an audience.

Another batch of names was called and the beautiful young woman she'd noticed earlier went to the stage. She was introduced as Sasha Fontenot and her choice of song was "I'm in Love with a Wonderful Guy." The girl opened her mouth to sing and Letti gasped at the purity and power of her voice.

Everyone else in the theater was equally stunned. Rachel was staring almost with her mouth open and Josh looked like the cat that swallowed the canary. She then delivered a few of Nellie's lines, and Letti detected the faintest of Cajun accents Sasha used to create Nellie's Arkansas twang. After singing like that, nothing, including an accent more Louisiana than Arkansas, was going to cost the new girl the role.

The auditions finally wrapped up. Rachel said they would call everyone soon and encouraged them to continue auditioning at the Durango. She and Kevin drifted toward the parking lot along with Vivienne and Miguel Abonce.

"You did great tonight, Letti," Vivienne enthused. "They'll cast you in a heartbeat. And Kevin, I can hardly wait to see you in that sailor suit."

"Thanks. I don't know that I did all that well."

"You did," Letti and Vivienne said in unison.

"I know jack about it and I was still impressed. Miguel Abonce," Miguel said, extending his hand to Kevin.

"Kevin Summerset." Kevin shook his hand enthusiastically. "You're the guy we have to thank for the new digs. My mom and dad sing your praises on a regular basis."

"Your parents are kind." Miguel smiled. "So, Letti, out of the black clothes and up on the stage?"

"I guess."

Vivienne looked at her. "You sound less than thrilled. Why did you try out for the role if you don't want it?"

Letti looked around and lowered her voice. "I was bribed. They told me if I'd take Bloody Mary, Sophie could play Liat. It would be good for her future. Her first role as an adult in an adult production. Josh tried to convince me that I'm the only one he has that can pull it off."

"You are," Vivienne said.

"At least right now," Miguel added. "If Vivi wasn't due to deliver, she could have done it beautifully."

"Yes, she could. But Vivi, would you even want to? You're way younger than the character."

"That's why they call it acting, honey. I would have done it in a heartbeat."

"If she's willing to play a green witch with flying monkeys and a mean mermaid in a mermaid tail, why wouldn't she do Bloody Mary?" Miguel asked.

"I would have rather had Nellie," Letti admitted.

"I know you would," Vivi said. "But that role's going to go to a girl in her twenties. Even I'm too old to play her." She bit her lip. "Letti, listen to me. If that's what's holding you back, the age thing, don't let it. You will be a wonderful Bloody Mary. Absolutely wonderful." She smiled encouragingly.

"She'll do it for Sophie, if for no other reason," Kevin piped up.

Kevin was right about that. She would do anything for her daughter, and Josh and Rachel knew it.

Letti whipped out her phone and scrolled down to Rachel's number. "I'll take it. Do I tell Sophie or wait until the formal announcement?"

"I'd say wait. The fewer who know about our deal, the better. And thanks," Rachel added. "You'll be great."

We'll see.

Chapter Eleven

Kevin whistled under his breath as he loaded the last of the sodas into the refrigerator. Tonight was the dress rehearsal of the adult production of *The Little Mermaid* and Josh wanted cold drinks and snacks for the newspaper critics. The cast and crew were exhausted, but the excitement was almost palpable as they rehearsed one more time before the curtain went up for the public.

In some ways, tonight was as important as opening night since every critic in town who reviewed Durango productions would be in attendance. Letti had been on a high all week as she whipped her crew into shape.

"They're good," she said last night as they shared a gooey late-night plate of tacos and craft beer at Thirties. "The sets are more complicated than I expected them to be."

He went through both restrooms with a cleaning brush and was vacuuming the lobby carpet when Rachel spotted him. She motioned him over to the concession stand and handed him a ten. "The usual?" he asked.

"Two of everything. Josh and I won't get out of here until late. We need something to hold us." He handed her two cokes and two candy bars. "Thanks. Did Josh ever text you about *South Pacific*?"

"You mean did he let me know I'm playing Joseph Cable? He did. A couple of days ago."

"Not that there was ever any doubt. Your audition was wonderful."

"Thanks." He looked up and spotted Letti and Sophie coming in the lobby. Both were dressed in the crew's usual head-to-toe black and they both looked tired. They spotted him and Rachel and detoured to the concession stand.

"Can I get you ladies anything?" he asked.

Letti handed him a twenty. "Diet Sprite and popcorn for me. Whatever Sophie wants."

Sophie looked over at him with eyes that were hooded. "Pepsi and a couple of Snickers."

"Coming right up."

He wondered what was going on behind Sophie's bland expression. Letti told him she'd laid down the law about Sophie's attitude. In a way he could understand her daughter's feelings. But Letti was right. If Sophie was willing to accept her father and Wade, she could accept him and her mother. He handed Sophie her drink and candy bars and scooped Letti a bag of popcorn.

Sophie thanked him before turning to Rachel. "Thanks for casting me in *South Pacific*," she said politely. "I'm looking forward to doing it."

"Your first adult production," Rachel enthused.

"Well, the first where I have an adult role," Sophie said. "I was in a few adult productions when they needed a child. I was Jane one time in *Mary Poppins,* and one of the orphans in *Oliver.*"

"And she played Molly the first time the Durango did *Annie,*" Letti said proudly.

"Quite a résumé," Kevin said.

"I guess," Sophie responded diffidently.

Kevin was surprised. He'd expect a lot more enthusiasm than that.

"Are you helping your mom tonight?" Rachel asked.

Sophie nodded. "Two of her crew members called in sick. One of my Academy friends is coming too. Mom bribed me with a pair of fancy *chanklas* I've been lusting after." She raised her hand and waved at a girl coming in the door. "Cindy. Over here."

The girls disappeared into the auditorium. Letti bit her lip as she watched them go. "I thought she'd be more excited. Her first grown-up role in an adult production."

"Well, I'm excited to get her. I'm excited to get you both." Rachel winked.

"Thanks."

They chatted a few more minutes before Letti went backstage and Rachel greeted the first critic of the night.

Kevin frowned as he finished vacuuming the carpet. Sophie wasn't the only one who was a little "off" tonight. Letti didn't seem like herself either. He didn't presume to be an expert, but by now he knew her well enough to know that something was bothering her.

They had a tentative date tonight after the rehearsal, depending on whether the kids stayed with Owen and Wade. If they got to go on their date, he'd talk to her then.

Rachel and Josh treated the critics to popcorn and candy and sodas and escorted them to the auditorium. Kevin slipped in as the overture ended and sat down in the back row, and was impressed. The rehearsal went off without a hitch, and the critics were singing their praises as they walked out the door.

He freshened the lobby and the restrooms and waited patiently in the back while Miranda met with the cast and crew and went through a list of notes she'd made during the performance. He ducked out the back door and was waiting beside Letti's crossover when she came out minutes later.

She greeted him with a chaste kiss on the cheek. "You deserve better, but we have an audience."

He looked around at the packed parking lot. "Let's go someplace a little less crowded. Got any ideas?"

"Marco's at his dad's place and Sophie's having a sleepover with Cindy. My house?"

"Works for me."

He followed her to her comfortable two-story home in an older subdivision of spacious ranch houses and oak trees. He'd come to the door a couple of times and been as far as the living room once, but this was the first time he got to see the rest of the house.

The family room and kitchen were awash with light and color. Brightly decorated Talavera tile graced the kitchen walls, and Saltillo tile flooring in the kitchen and family room.

The family room sofa and chairs were attractive yet sturdy, with bright canvas cushions striped in the same colors as the kitchen tile. A big-screen TV was mounted above the fireplace, and bookshelves were chock full of family pictures dating back to her children's births.

To her credit, she displayed pictures of the kids with Owen, and even a few of the four of them, taken when the children were much younger. He leaned over and peered at one taken maybe ten years ago of them at the beach.

"He was a handsome bastard before he got hurt," Letti observed as she looked over his shoulder. "With that makeup Wade's mother fixed him up with, he still looks that way from the stage." She gestured to the picture. "I was a hell of a lot prettier then too."

"No prettier than you are now, Letti. Younger is younger, but you were stunning then and you are now."

"You have an hour and a half to stop saying things like that," she deadpanned.

"But it's true," he protested. "You are every bit as beautiful today as you were then. Honestly."

"Thanks." Her smile was small. "I don't know about you, but I'm hungry. I have leftover casserole in the fridge, or we can make sandwiches."

"What kind of casserole?"

"Chili with corn tortillas and cheese."

"Sounds good."

Letti nuked them generous portions and served them with bagged salad and cold beer. Letti could cook. They talked, but whatever was on her mind at the theater was still bothering her.

After they'd cleaned up the kitchen and loaded the dishwasher, he asked, "What's wrong?"

She turned to him with a breezy smile. "Absolutely nothing."

"Bullshit."

She bit her lip and her face turned red. "You have to kiss Sophie."

"What?"

"You have to kiss Sophie," she said a little louder.

"What do you mean, I have to kiss Sophie?"

"You know what I mean. You're playing Joseph. She's playing Liat. You have to *kiss her* in the play."

"Oh." He shrugged. "So?" He didn't bother to hide his confusion.

"I don't like it." She looked put out. "It's silly, I know. But the thought of you and her…" She shook her head.

"Me and her what?"

"There's an *eww* factor. You might not feel that way. She's young and beautiful."

"She's a young and beautiful *child,* Letti. Yes, she's playing an adult role. But the bottom line is that she's still seventeen years old. I haven't been into seventeen-year-old girls since I was seventeen."

He looked at her as the truth dawned on him. "Is this some more of the age thing?"

She sighed. "I guess so. I already feel old playing Bloody Mary, and then the thought of you kissing Sophie, even if it's Joseph kissing Liat…it bothers me."

Okay. Time for damage control. "*Joseph* is kissing *Liat*. Kevin is *not* kissing Sophie. Kevin doesn't *want* to kiss Sophie. Kevin *wants* to kiss Letti, the woman that I and every other man in the theater lusts after. Only I'm the lucky one who gets her." He held out his arms. "Come here and I'll show you how much I want to do that."

Letti smiled for real this time and moved into his arms.

***

Kevin said exactly what she needed to hear.

Letti melted into his arms as Kevin's lips lowered onto hers.

He wanted her. It was a heady feeling knowing she turned him on the way she did. She wrapped her arms around his waist and kissed him back, taking and giving in equal measure.

Her heart pounded and she trembled in his arms. Her senses sharpened. Her pulse soared in anticipation. They'd had sex a lot by now. Somehow, every time was better than the time before.

When he raised his head, he rasped, "Did I make my point?"

"Nope. Not convinced. You need to work at it."

"My pleasure."

Before she could object, he swept her off her feet and proceeded to climb the stairs with her in his arms. "Kevin, for crying out loud. Put me down. You're gonna give yourself a hernia."

"Nah, you're not that heavy." He carried her up the stairs and down the hall. "Which one's yours?"

"Second room on the left."

He carried her into her bedroom and put her down gently on the bed. He sat down beside her and looked around. "Beautiful room. Very feminine. Very you."

She flicked her eyes around the room at the deep rose comforter and drapes and flowered throw pillows. "I redid the whole thing after Owen moved out."

"I kind of like it. But then I like everything about you." He kicked off his shoes and pulled his tee over his head. "But I guess you know that already." He stood long enough to shuck his shorts and briefs and stood in front of her with his hands on his hips and his erection jutting out in front of him. "Do I need to help you?"

"Nah. Just taking a minute to enjoy the view."

"Maybe I'd like to enjoy the view as well."

She smirked. Then made short work of stripping.

He held her by the shoulders as his gaze traveled the length of her banging body. He'd taken her in many times in the last month, but each time felt like the first as he admired her beauty.

He made no secret of the fact that he found her beautiful, that looking at her was a big fuckin' turn-on. She enjoyed his body, and openly scanned him frequently. She relished gazing at his nudity, his body hard and firm, his shoulders broad, his waist trim, and his washboard abs a delight.

But Letti was a tactile person and wanted to feast with her hands and her lips as well as her eyes. She reached out and ran her fingers through the tangle of hair covering his chest before following it down to where his cock rose.

"I like looking. I like touching even better."

"Touch all you like." He leaned down and planted a gentle kiss on her lips.

As one they moved to the bed, collapsing together in a tangle of arms and legs that had them laughing.

They spent long minutes kissing and caressing one another. Now that they knew each other's likes and dislikes, they both tripped each other's buttons, and their knowledge heightened their pleasure.

She knew he loved to kiss her nipples, and he knew she loved it when he did. She knew he loved for her to caress his cock, but he didn't like it when she played with his navel. He knew she loved for him to put his fingers inside her, but didn't much like for him to play with her toes. He knew she loved for him to go down on her. She knew he loved her to reciprocate. They both loved for the other one to be on top, and neither of them could get enough kissing.

As had become their way, they took their time. Kevin kissed his way down her body, paying special attention to her sensitive nipples.

Letti gasped as his lips teased and tortured one nipple at the same time his fingers found and caressed her other sensitive bud. He took his time, using her delighted gasps as a measure of her pleasure to drive her higher and higher, until she arched her back and convulsed around his fingers deep inside her.

His lips traveled lower and he pushed her legs farther open. "I love making you come," he murmured as his lips found her clit, and he worked his magic. She spiraled again, crying out as a second wave of pleasure overtook her, followed by a third. He slid up her body and reached down for his wallet. "Oh, hell. I'm out of condoms. You have any?"

"No. We used the last of mine Saturday night." Letti lay back on the pillow.

"It's okay. A little creativity and a great blow job go a long way." He grinned at her wickedly.

"When were you tested last?"

"I went in the Monday after our weekend at the lake. After I knew we were going to continue seeing one another. What about you?"

"Part of my physical in March and I haven't been with anyone but you since."

"Are you on the pill?"

Letti hesitated. "Actually, no. I've already started menopause. I won't get pregnant."

Kevin looked at her disbelievingly. "You're not that old."

"The women in my family don't have to be. Mom and *Abuela* were about my age."

"Oh." An odd expression crossed his face. If Letti didn't know better, she'd think he was disappointed. Then he leaned forward and took her lips in a long, lingering kiss. "If we don't have anything to worry about, then ungloved it is."

They kissed, and Letti could taste herself on his tongue. Kevin moved between her legs and entered her in a swift thrust. "Damn. That feels so good," he murmured as he began to move inside her. "So much more intense."

She met him, thrust for thrust. By now Letti knew she would always come with Kevin inside of her. So she let herself feel as they chased the high.

It felt wonderful having nothing between them, their bodies more intimately connected than they had ever been. She cried out as the powerful orgasm overtook her, shaking her to her core. Kevin threw his head back and arched into her, his seed shooting deep within her body as he groaned his pleasure.

They clung together for long moments. He brushed the hair back from her face. "That has to be the most awesome ever. I didn't know."

"Didn't know what?"

"What it feels like with no condom. Or maybe it's you. Maybe it was that wonderful because it was you."

"Or maybe it was that wonderful because it was you," she said softly.

"Us. It was us."

They continued to hold one another. Kevin finally withdrew and lay on his back with his arm around her. She snuggled up to his chest. "I've missed you in my bed," he said. "Every night since the weekend at the lake. I like having you next to me when I sleep."

"I like it too."

She draped her arm across his stomach. He dropped off to sleep almost immediately. She was tired, and at the same time delightfully sated. Still, sleep didn't come easily. She was all too aware of the man she clung to in the dark. His voice. His touch. His smile. Everything about him called out to her. It was supposed to be a fling. A short-term thing, strictly for fun. Nothing serious, nothing permanent.

She knew what a fling felt like. And this was no mere fling.

She was falling for him. She was falling hard for the man curled up beside her.

Sooner or later she was going to get hurt.

But somehow she couldn't bring herself to care.

***

Kevin lay awake in the dim light of early morning. Pink rays filtered through the drapes covering Letti's bedroom window. The alarm clock said six. Not that it mattered. Letti's morning class didn't start until ten and it was doubtful that the kids would be here anytime soon. He should turn over and grab another couple of hours of sleep. He and Letti would be at the theater until late tonight. She needed her sleep, and if he got up to leave he risked waking her.

He turned away from the woman sleeping peacefully beside him. They had gotten separated in the night, but she was still close enough that he could feel the warmth of her body and smell the combination of her shampoo and her tangy essence. The fragrance called to him like a siren song, demanding and seductive. But everything about her called to him. Her face. Her body. Her voice. Her sassy smile. Her personality. The way she cared about those around her. The way she fiercely protected her own.

Everything about her appealed to him.

Which should have made him happier than it did.

He shut his eyes and tried to go back to sleep. But rest was elusive. Instead of drifting off, he kept replaying last night's conversation in his head. Menopause. She said she was going through menopause. It didn't seem like it was a big deal to her. She'd been matter of fact, clinical even, in explaining why they could go without a condom. The loss of fertility didn't seem to bother her.

But it bothered him. It bothered him a lot.

Because he was falling for her, big time. To the point that he'd had more than one fantasy about defying convention and marrying her. He'd imagined her pregnant with his child. Lots of women her age had children and he'd assumed she could as well. He'd imagined them raising a family together. She would teach and he would go to work for the family law firm. They would do shows together at the Durango. They would watch their children grow up enjoying the benefits of having Sophie and Marco as their older siblings. He and Letti would have the family he'd imagined.

But if she was already going through menopause, that wouldn't happen with her. If he married her, his dreams of children of his own would never come true.

He wasn't sure he was willing to give up on the life he'd wanted ever since he knew what a family was.

But he wasn't willing to give up Letti, either.

There was no way he could turn his back on her. There was no way he could let go of what they had. He might be young, but he wasn't stupid. What they shared didn't come along every day. Maybe once or twice in a lifetime, if a person was lucky. He wasn't about to let go of that special something the two of them created together.

He couldn't bear the thought of letting her go.

Chapter Twelve

Letti pulled into the Durango parking lot. She and Sophie were due in less than ten minutes for *South Pacific* rehearsals and neither wanted to be late. Heat waves shimmered off the newly poured asphalt and the smell of tar seeped into the car despite the rolled-up windows.

The sun was low in the sky, but the city was coping with a July heat wave that had air conditioners running full blast and young and old alike buried up to their necks in the swimming pools around town. Sophie and Marco had spent the better part of the afternoon at the neighborhood swim club while Letti sat with her feet propped on the coffee table memorizing Bloody Mary's lines.

Rehearsals for *South Pacific* had begun last week, and between the weeknight rehearsals and the weekend performances of *The Little Mermaid,* Letti's evenings were full. She was teaching her daytime class at the college, taking care of her family between all her obligations, and when she got to sleep, she dropped off immediately.

Getting together with Kevin was a challenge.

But they managed to spend the night at her house when the kids were with Owen and Wade, and steal a couple of hours here and there at his carriage house apartment when they weren't.

And it wasn't all sex. Kevin had come over for dinner with her and the kids more than once, and they'd gotten together with the theater crowd at Thirties for after-show dinner. Sophie was still wary, but Kevin and Marco had hit it off. Letti's theater friends were good with her and Kevin as a couple. Her mother and grandmother weren't pleased, but they weren't going to be, and after Letti laid down the law they'd been grudgingly polite about it. Right now, life was good. Better than it had been for the last five years.

Though, she wasn't all that sure about *South Pacific*. Or her role in the play. She was beginning to regret the deal to play the wily merchant making a living off the American sailors.

Bloody Mary was not coming to life. And she couldn't put her finger on the reason.

She and Sophie got out of the car and hustled across the hot, smelly asphalt. Rachel, who was directing, handed them each a rehearsal schedule for the week. Letti and Sophie were scheduled to rehearse with Kevin this evening—Letti first, and Sophie later.

Sophie thanked Rachel for the schedule and disappeared in the direction of her assigned rehearsal room. "We're doing the first scene with your character," Rachel said. "When Joe meets Bloody Mary for the first time. If we get far enough, we'll run you through 'Bali Ha'i.' Kevin and Owen are waiting for you in the dance studio." Despite his upcoming wedding, Owen had gone ahead and agreed to play Luther Billis, a fairly major role.

She found Kevin and Owen and some of the ensemble sailors in the medium-sized Academy studio. Owen and the ensemble were already rehearsing, singing "There is Nothing Like a Dame." Kevin was sitting cross-legged on the floor next to the wall. He patted the floor beside him and she sank down.

"You may have to pull me up," she told him.

He smiled at her. "Not a problem." He looked from her to Owen. "How weird is this? You're acting with both your ex and your current."

"Also with my ex's future. I have a scene or two with Wade. And you have to kiss my daughter. I'm still trying to get past that."

"Actually, we rehearsed the scene with Rachel last week. No biggie. Your daughter handled it like the pro that she is."

"She's something else." Letti smiled with delight. "She's going to the top, Kevin. I can feel it in my bones."

"I don't doubt that for a minute."

Owen and the sailors finished their song. Rachel came in and briefly discussed the scene with them. Then Letti and Kevin ran through the first meeting of Joseph and Bloody Mary.

Letti had purchased a DVD of the old movie and spent hours listening to actress Juanita Hall's version of Bloody Mary's Pidgin English. After she'd read up on the character and learned that Bloody Mary is Tonkinese, she'd also gone to an accent website and listened to people speaking with Vietnamese accents and listened to how their English pronunciations differed from standard.

Rachel nodded when Letti ran through the first few lines of Bloody Mary's dialogue. "You're doing a good job with the accent. Kevin, try to sound a little more upper crust. Joseph's Main Line Philadelphia. He needs to sound like it."

"Oughta be easy for him. He's Main Line San Antonio," Owen poked.

"Main Line San Antonio sounds like J.R. Ewing," Kevin groused. "I gather you don't want J.R.?"

"Uh, no. Old Yankee money, Kevin," Rachel admonished. "Let's hear old Yankee money."

They laughed and Letti, Kevin and Owen got down to work. The ensemble laughed again when she delivered Bloody Mary's signature line to Joseph, "You sexy man." Eventually, the scene started coming together. At least it did with Kevin and Owen. Try as she might, her portrayal of Bloody Mary was missing something. She knew she wasn't doing that great a job. But she wasn't sure where she was missing the mark.

Rachel was a perfectionist, stopping them all the time, and they had not reached the point where Bloody Mary sang "Bali Ha'i" when Rachel called a halt. "Nice job, everybody. Letti, I don't have you scheduled for anything else this evening, but you're welcome to stay and see Sophie at work. Kevin, ten-minute break."

Letti almost excused herself. She had no desire to see Kevin and Sophie rehearse their roles as lovers. But curiosity and pride in her daughter won out, and she took a short restroom break. On her way back to the studio, she stopped for a minute and listened from the hall to Cameron and Sasha singing "Some Enchanted Evening," and chills ran down her spine. She had no idea how their chemistry would be. But if it was anywhere near as good as their singing, the two of them could carry the show and it wouldn't matter what anyone else did.

Sophie was already in the rehearsal room with Kevin. Letti leaned against the wall out of the way. Rachel was taking Sophie and Kevin through the scene the morning after Joseph and Liat had made love. It was a sweet scene, tender, and seriously politically incorrect in today's climate, with a native teenager and a Navy lieutenant having sex. But under Rachel's direction, Kevin and Sophie made it work.

Letti swelled with pride as she watched her daughter bring the tender, sensitive Liat to life, mostly with her expressive eyes and face, since Liat spoke no English and Sophie had only a few lines.

Her daughter had what it took. She was going to be wonderful in her chosen profession. She would make a success of an acting career.

Letti's little girl was going to be a star.

It was late before Rachel was satisfied. Sophie gathered up her stuff and ducked out. Kevin gave Letti a sweet kiss and said he would see her tomorrow. She was about to make her getaway when Rachel stopped her.

"Can we talk for a couple of minutes?"

"Sure."

Rachel gestured to a couple of chairs along the wall. They sat and Rachel took a deep breath. "Bloody Mary's not coming to life the way she needs to."

"Like I don't know that?" Letti snapped. "I'm at a loss. I've memorized the lines. I've researched the accent. I've read commentaries and analyses of the character. I've watched the movie and a pilfered copy of a recording made of the stage play. I'm trying."

"I know you're trying. But at the same time, you're holding back. You're not letting her come to life."

Letti's eyes narrowed. "What do you mean, I'm holding back?"

Rachel sighed. "You don't really want to play Bloody Mary, and it's ruining your performance."

"No, I don't want to play her. She's old."

"She's the mother of a teenager. You're the mother of a teenager." Rachel straightened her shoulders. "Letti, come on. You need to get over wanting to play the ingénue. It's not gonna happen anymore, and you need to accept it. You can either bemoan the younger roles we're not going to cast you in, or you can sink your teeth into the ones written for an actress your age. You need to get over feeling like those roles are beneath you. You need to cut loose and bring those characters to life the way they deserve to be seen."

"I told you I'm trying. But most actresses do play younger. Sometimes a lot younger."

"Tell that to Meryl Streep. Her roles have aged along with her." Rachel looked at Letti with frustration. "You could be the best actress in the theater if you'd let go. *Please*, Letti. Bloody Mary's one of the most important characters in the play. Please do her justice," Rachel pleaded.

"I'm sorry. I'm not trying to shortchange the role."

"The thing is, Bloody Mary's like you," Rachel said softly. "She would do anything for her daughter. She's desperately trying to give the girl a better life. Exactly like you're trying to do for Sophie. Do some digging there. She's inside of you, Letti. Let her out."

Rachel patted Letti on the arm and got up and left.

Letti walked slowly to the car. *Bloody Mary's like me.* It took Letti all the way home to wrap her head around that thought. But Rachel was right. As misguided as Bloody Mary's attempts to pawn Liat off on Joseph might be, the woman's heart was in the right place. She was willing to do anything and everything for her child. She thought marriage to an American serviceman would get her daughter a better life, and she did everything she could to see that happen.

Actually, Letti understood Bloody Mary quite well.

And understanding a character was crucial to bringing that character to life.

Marco was up in his room playing an online video game. Sophie disappeared into her bedroom, and Letti made a bowl of popcorn and sat down in front of the TV.

The DVD of *South Pacific* was already in the player. She hit the "Play" button, and this time she watched the character. Sure, Bloody Mary was funny. But at the same time, her love for her daughter and her desire to see the girl marry well was poignant. And her bravery was touching, as she battled the prejudice that surrounded her and her people.

Rachel was right. Letti had been phoning it in. It was time to get real.

Bloody Mary was a compelling character who deserved to be fully brought to life.

Letti finally felt prepared to do that.

***

Letti was knocking Bloody Mary out of the ballpark.

Kevin couldn't be prouder of her.

He sat on the floor and listened as Owen and Letti rehearsed the scene with Bloody Mary, Billis, and the French girls on the beach of Bali Ha'i. Kevin hadn't gotten to sit back and watch her work all that much. Joseph was in almost every scene of Bloody Mary's. Rehearsing with her had been a pleasure. Letti was bringing the wily merchant to life. Rather than capitalizing on the comic aspects of the character, Letti's Bloody Mary was driven by the desire to see to her daughter's welfare by any means at her disposal. Her version of Bloody Mary was at once fierce and poignant, a woman it was impossible not to admire. He'd been a little worried at first. Letti's early rehearsals had been lackluster. But then it was like a light had gone on. Letti had walked into the rehearsal room and suddenly the character came to life in front of their eyes.

She was that good.

She and Owen finished the scene and Rachel came back with several suggestions. They ran through the scene again and Kevin resisted the urge to roll his eyes. They had been in rehearsals for almost a month and had another to go before tech week and Rachel was acting like the production was tomorrow. He sat and quietly observed as Letti and Owen went back through the scene implementing Rachel's suggestions. Rather, he watched Letti. Her face, her voice, her sexy body in the yoga pants and tee she liked to rehearse in. He didn't watch her, he drank in the sight of her. He couldn't tear his eyes off the woman who was beginning to mean everything to him.

Which scared the shit out of him.

He was falling in love with a woman who couldn't make his dream of a family with children come true.

Kevin sighed and leaned his head against the wall. Letti was everything he'd ever wanted in a life partner. Yet, she was not. It took two people to create that family he wanted so badly. Him, and a wife who could carry and give birth to his children. If he stuck to his timetable, he wouldn't even be able to think about a family for several more years. Even if she could still get pregnant now, she most likely wouldn't be able to by then.

He found himself torn. Did he give up his relationship with Letti, or did he give up on the family he'd wanted all his life?

If he was forced to make the decision tonight, he wasn't sure what he would do.

But he didn't have to decide tonight.

He would have to decide at some point, however. Sometime soon. The longer he waited, the more deeply he was going to fall in love with her, and the harder it would be to let her go.

Owen and Letti ran through the scene two more times and called it quits. He stood up and planted a gentle kiss on her lips. "Good job tonight. Both of you."

"Don't I get a kiss too?" Owen teased, breaking into laughter when Kevin took a step back.

"I don't think so, darlin'," Letti shot back. "You have your own hunk at home to kiss. But I have to admit it's a pleasure to work with you again."

"I noticed how flawlessly the two of you play off each other," Kevin said. "Lots of practice."

"We used to act together all the time," Owen said. "Now that I can cover the scars with that wonderful makeup, I'm guessing we'll be cast in the same production every so often." He looked from Letti to Kevin. "But I have to admit the two of you have good chemistry together as well."

"Why, thank you." Owen's praise warmed Kevin's heart.

They were gathering their things when Rachel came running into the room carrying a mermaid costume. "Vivi's gone into labor and can't do the shows this weekend. Letti, you said you were willing to play Ursula. Did you mean it?"

"I'd be willing, but I've never played the role before. I don't know the songs and I don't know the lines. Can't one of the Ursulas from the Academy cast step in?"

"The high school Ursula flew to Disney World. And the girl from the middle school production's too small and immature looking. The songs are easy and we can hide copies of the script in the scenery. Sophie will help you prepare. Please, Letti. It's only three more performances and I'll pay for your drinks at Thirties for an entire year if you'll do it for us."

"Double my pay," Letti said, deadpan. "In addition to the drinks."

"Done."

"Since none of us get a plug nickel for acting, that's an empty promise," Owen said.

"I don't know. It will cost her if I'm drinking on her tab for a year," Letti responded. "I'll do it. When did Vivi go into labor? She's not due for another month."

"I don't know. She called on the way to the hospital. Said her water broke so it wasn't a false alarm. She sounded as cool as a cucumber. Miguel, not so much."

Owen and Letti looked at one another and laughed. "Sounds about right," Owen said.

"You were a basket case both times," Letti teased.

Owen looked at her with affection. "And both times you were an absolute trooper."

A sharp stab of jealousy took Kevin by surprise. On some level he knew that Owen and Letti shared a lot of history and memories. Of course they would share the memory of their children's births. A memory he would never get to share with her.

He would never rush her to the hospital in labor with his son or daughter. They would never lean over together, cooing at a sleeping newborn. They would never give a birthday party together or go to open house at the elementary school. All memories she shared with Owen and would never share with him.

The thought hurt.

Rachel hustled Letti off so she could try on the costume. Owen left with Wade. Kevin's car was in the parking lot, but he waited around anyway. Letti and Rachel came out of Rachel's office fifteen minutes later giggling like schoolgirls.

"She rocks the costume," Rachel crowed.

"I can barely breathe in the thing," Letti complained.

"I thought Vivi was wearing a big costume to accommodate the bump," Kevin said.

"Ah, but Miss Foxy here can fit into the high school costume from the Academy production," Rachel said. "Now, you have the script and the CD to practice with. I'll have your cheat sheets to hide in the scenery ready to go tomorrow. You and the crew can figure out where you want them when you set up tomorrow. Anything else?"

"A few coffee pods would be nice. I'll be up all night learning my lines."

"I'll have fresh coffee on when you get here tomorrow." Rachel reached out and hugged Letti. "You're a lifesaver."

"No problem. Let me know the minute the baby arrives. Do we know if it's a boy or girl?"

"If they know they're not telling. Now get out of here and learn some songs. You have a mermaid to play." Rachel made a shooing motion with her hands.

Kevin walked Letti to her car. Even though it was after ten, they were deep into August and the air was still hot. "I guess this means I'm not getting laid," he muttered.

"'Fraid not." She tilted her head and stared at him. "Is something bothering you tonight?"

Yes, something's bothering me. You can't give me the family I want.

Kevin bit his lip. No way was he going to admit that to her. She already was sensitive about her age. No way was he going to add to that. Instead, he took her in his arms and planted a passionate kiss on her lips. "That's what's bothering me. You look good enough to eat and you have a date with a mermaid and a crab."

She looked at him doubtfully. "It's not only that."

"It is," he argued, hoping he sounded convincing. "I'm spoiled and horny for my woman."

She laughed. "All right, then." She stood on her tiptoes and kissed him again. "There's always Sunday. The matinee's over by five."

"Sunday can't come soon enough."

They shared another deep, wet kiss and then he watched her drive off.

He drove straight home and threw back a couple of beers before curling up in bed. His rest was interrupted by vivid dreams he was powerless to stop. Dreams of rocking a dark-haired baby in his arms, of pushing a little boy on a park swing, of sitting in the audience cheering on a little girl's first stage role. Dreams of holding a woman's hand while a handsome young man received a diploma. Dreams of everything he couldn't have if it was Letti was by his side.

Chapter Thirteen

Juliana Elizabeth Abonce was the image of her daddy.

Letti smiled down at the beautiful little girl and made kissy noises. "Aren't you the prettiest little thing?" she cooed at the sleeping infant. "You look like your daddy, yes you do, little one." She straightened and winced at the catch in her back. "She's absolutely gorgeous, Vivi. Good size for a baby as early as she is." The baby weighed in at seven pounds even.

"Wel-l-l, the doctor thinks I might have miscalculated a bit. I may have already been pregnant when I had that last light period," Vivi admitted.

"Or Julie might be a really big kid," Miguel added. "Vivi's father was even taller than Cameron, which put him at six-three or four. I always felt like a pre-teen next to him." He leaned over the bassinet. "She's beautiful, though. If I say so myself."

Kevin looked puzzled. "Aren't all newborns beautiful?"

"No," Letti and Vivienne said in unison.

"They're not?"

"Not even," Miguel added. "He's cute now, but my nephew Jeremy was the homeliest kid I ever saw. Even his father admitted it."

"Those are the babies we call 'sweet' or 'darling' or 'adorable,'" Letti explained. "My Sophie was beautiful like Julie, but we got a lot of 'sweet' and 'darling' and 'adorable' with Marco at first."

Vivienne smiled. "He certainly grew out of it."

"That he did. He gets three or four phone calls a day from girls." She mock-shuddered. "It was bad enough when Sophie developed sex appeal. I wasn't ready for it to happen to Marco, too." She leaned over. "Oh, look. She's waking up. Is she ready for a feeding?"

"Probably." Vivienne's smile faded. "Miguel, will you warm her a bottle?" She looked down at her hands. "I'm not making enough milk. The doctor put her on formula yesterday." She wiped a tear from her cheek. "I feel like a bad mother."

"Don't you dare feel like that," Miguel said fiercely. "You're a fantastic mother." He looked over at Letti and Kevin. "Her mom and grandmother were the same way." He headed toward the kitchen.

"He's right. You tried, yes? So give yourself credit for having enough sense to acknowledge that she needs formula and don't worry about it," Letti said firmly.

"Yes, Mom." Vivi popped a salute.

Letti volunteered to change Julie's diaper while Miguel warmed the bottle. She picked up the baby to hand to Vivi, but to her surprise Kevin reached out his arms. "Let me," he said quietly. "I know how. Renee would let me give Emma a bottle now and then."

Vivi nodded and Letti handed the baby over to Kevin. "You must have been mighty young at the time," she said.

He settled the baby into his arms. "I was nine." He took the bottle from Miguel and eased it into Julie's mouth, giving the baby a minute to latch on. "That's right, little one. It's good, isn't it?" he crooned. "Pretty baby. Pretty, pretty little girl."

Vivi and Miguel looked at Letti with surprise. "Who would have thought?" Vivi murmured.

"He's really good with her," Miguel breathed softly.

Letti's heart sank as she watched Kevin with the baby. He was a natural. From the looks of it, he'd be a wonderful father. And there was longing in his eyes as he looked down at the baby in his arms. It couldn't be any clearer. He wanted a family someday.

A family that she couldn't give him.

Letti fought back the urge to cry. She'd be damned if she let her tears ruin their visit with Vivi and Miguel. But she and Kevin would have to talk.

She shoved her emotions aside for the time being and instead indulged in a trip down memory lane, dispensing bits of hard-earned parenting wisdom to her friends. They in turn shared their plans to build a big house on the edge of town. It would be three times the size of their current condo and have a big play area in the backyard.

Julie drank most of the bottle and delivered a noisy belch on Kevin's shoulder. Letti caught Kevin's eye and he handed the baby to Vivienne.

"We've taken up enough of your time," she said. "Cardinal rule number one. When she naps, you do too. We'll get out of your hair so you can do that."

"The nap might have to wait a bit," Vivienne said. "Jessica texted that she and Brian are on their way over with a gift. I doubt they'll be long, though. They both have to work this afternoon."

They said their goodbyes and took the elevator down, only to meet Jessica and Brian on ground level. Brian was clutching a balloon with a card tied to the end of the ribbon and they were holding hands and smiling broadly.

"What have you been up to that put smiles like those on your face?" Kevin wiggled his eyebrows up and down.

"I wish," Brian laughed. "We just left the jewelry store. Show 'em, Jess."

She let go of his hand and held hers up to the light. Sparkling diamonds surrounded a deep blue sapphire. "The sapphire's to go with her eyes. She's gonna marry me," Brian said proudly.

Letti squealed and enveloped Jessica in a huge hug. "Congratulations. I'm so happy for you."

Kevin shook Brian's hand. "Way to go. You caught yourself a mighty pretty lady."

"When's the wedding?" Letti asked. "Christmas? Next summer?"

Jessica's face turned red and Brian smiled sheepishly. "As soon as she and her mother can put something together," he said.

"I'm looking at A-line wedding dresses," Jessica admitted. "I don't want to look too pregnant when I walk down the aisle. Not that anybody cares about that but me."

Letti giggled in spite of herself. "Ah, yes. And I guess you'll be wanting gift certificates for the baby store at your bridal shower. Lord, speaking of a shower, has anyone at the theater said anything about giving you one?"

"Not yet. You two are the first to know."

"Congratulations for a second time," Letti said. "And we'll put together a party. You really do have a lot to celebrate."

Jessica looked at Brian with love in her eyes. "We do. We sure do."

They got in the elevator. Kevin stared after them wistfully as the doors closed.

Oh yeah, they needed to talk.

He took her hand and walked her to his car. "Are you free this afternoon?"

She nodded. "Sophie's at the Academy and Marco has an all-day band practice at school. It's hard to imagine school starts in a week and a half. Mine too."

He nodded. "I'm going in for an all-day orientation tomorrow."

"Are you excited to be going back to school?"

"I find the subject matter fascinating. But I'm not looking forward to the long hours of study."

Letti said, "It's been my observation over the years that the more interesting the subject matter, the less onerous the time required to learn it."

"Good point."

The ride to Letti's was mostly silent. He followed her into the house. She moved aside when he went to take her into his arms. "Come upstairs with me. We need to talk."

"I guess we do." He took her hand and followed her up the stairs. Still holding hands, they sat down on the side of the bed.

"Tell me what you're thinking," she prompted softly.

He turned to her and there were tears in his eyes. "I want what they have. I want a family, Letti. I want a wife and a couple of little kids to come home to. Does that make me a monster?"

"God, no, Kevin. That makes you a wonderful man who wants what most men want sooner or later. Even if they don't realize it when they're your age. The difference is that you know it now."

"I've known it since I was nine years old. I'd hold Emma and tell myself that someday I'd have a little baby like her. A wife and a pretty little baby."

Letti swallowed the lump in her throat. "You should have that, Kevin. A pretty little baby, maybe two or three of them. You'll have that, I promise."

"But you said you can't have any more babies. That you can't get pregnant anymore."

"I can't." She gripped his hand and willed the tears not to fall. "Someone else will have those babies with you. Someone who can carry those little ones and give birth to them." She bit her lip as the first tear rolled down her cheek. "We need to call this off. We need to stop seeing one another, before we get in so deep that we can't."

"I don't want to do that. I love you. We can have a few more months together, maybe even a year or two."

"A few more months or a year or two more to keep falling deeper and deeper in love? Is that really what we want?" She ran her hand down her arm. "This is killing us today. How do you think it's going to feel after a few more months or a year? By then, we may not be able to call it off."

"Would that be so bad?"

She looked him in the eye. "*Think,* Kevin. Think about today. You don't simply want what they have. You long for it. How are you gonna feel five, ten years down the line as more and more of your friends are raising a family and you aren't? No car seats, no birthday parties, no sleepovers. You're going to have a deep hole in your heart. Sophie and Marco won't fill it. They're on their way out the door. It would be you and me and a houseful of unrealized dreams."

She stopped and took a breath. "It happened to me, Kevin. I didn't get to live the life of my dreams and I've always regretted it. I don't want that for you." She wiped a tear off her cheek. "I love you too much to do that to you. It would be kinder to let you go before I can't."

"Don't I get a say in this?"

"You do. Shut your eyes, Kevin, and think. Fast-forward fourteen or fifteen years. You're forty years old. You've been in practice for over ten years. You're making nice money. You've worked hard and are achieving your professional goals. Now picture yourself coming home at the end of the day. You pull up in the driveway of your big, sprawling ranch house. You spot your neighbor's son and a couple of his friends shooting hoops. It hurts to see those kids, because you don't have that. You get out of the car and come into a quiet house and your fifty-five-year-old wife. That is, if our relationship has even survived the disappointment you would feel by then."

She gave it a minute to sink in. "Is that where you want to be in fifteen years? Or do you want to come home to someone shooting hoops in your driveway and a houseful of the noise only kids can generate?"

"Shit." He looked up. There was a mountain of regret in his expression. "You're right. I want the second picture."

"I love you, and I know you feel the same. But I can't have your babies. If I could, I'd say to hell with the age difference and go for it. But I can't, and I'll be damned if I rob you of the life you deserve."

"What do we do?" Kevin wiped a tear from his cheek.

"We make love one more time. We give each other that much. Then you go one way and I go the other."

"I hate this."

"So do I. But it's the only option if you're ever to have that family you've always wanted." She stood up and stripped off her tee. "Make love to me one more time, Kevin, so I can let you go."

They stared at one another while they slowly removed their clothes one piece at a time. When they were finally naked, they surveyed each other for a few minutes before moving slowly into one another's arms.

Letti breathed in the aroma of his soap and shampoo, and the unique essence that was Kevin. They held one another for long minutes before she raised her face for his kiss. "Love me, Kevin," she murmured as he lowered his face to hers. "Love me like I've never been loved before."

She moaned as his lips found hers. Their kiss was tender at first. But as the moments passed and passion overtook them, her heart beat faster and his breathing deepened. But there was more to their closeness. So much more than physical passion. There was love in their embrace, which made each touch and caress a thing of beauty.

They held each other for long moments, each loath to hurry, as they savored this bittersweet time together. They kissed and clung to one another, taking their sweet, sweet time. Then Kevin moved them to the bed and eased her down, joining her there and winding his arms around her neck. "I love you, baby. I love you so damned much."

She stared into his eyes. "I love you too. So damned much."

He covered her body with his own, kissing her long and hard before beginning the last exploration of her body that he would ever make. Her earlobes, her neck, her breasts, he paid tender homage to each. Her nipples tightened as he kissed and touched them. His touch was more than a physical experience. She could feel his love for her, and made her feel things she'd never felt before, not even with him.

He nibbled his way down her body, his lips first on her navel and then lower. His cock thrust upward against her calf, as he gently parted her legs. Letti trembled at the power of his touch as he found the center of her. He caressed her clit gently at first, but then with more passion as she began to spiral out of control until she finally broke and waves of love and passion cascaded all around her.

Not content with one outpouring of his love, he gave her some down time, and then began loving her again, his touch almost leisurely as he slowly coaxed her to another pulse-pounding height. This time the cascade was slower in coming, but sharper in its intensity.

She gasped and moaned and tried to sit up, but he pushed her down in the bedclothes. "One more, Letti. I want to give it to you one more time."

She laid back to let him work his magic as he wrung every bit of passion from her body with not one, but two more heart-stopping climaxes that had her screaming out his name. Then he rose up and entered her in a single swift thrust.

Tears ran down his handsome face as he rocked above her, slowly at first, but then faster and harder. Letti's passion swelled one more time, until they came together for the last time.

He kissed her so gently before turning them onto their sides, not pulling away even as his cock softened within her body.

They stared wordlessly, neither bothering to hide the emotion tearing them apart. The minutes ticked by. Finally Kevin pulled away and sat up.

"Is there any other way?" he asked brokenly.

She slid up and they sat side by side on the edge of the bed. "Not if you're going to have the family you always wanted. Kevin, I love you too much to deprive you of that. Go. Live out your dreams. Have the family you long for."

"What about you?"

What about her? She swallowed a huge lump in her throat. "I'll be okay. I have my children, my job, and the Durango."

He took her hand. "You'll find love again, Letti. I have to believe that."

She didn't think she'd find love again. She'd given her heart and soul to him, and right now, she wasn't sure she had it in her to open herself to that again. She bit back the remark that sprang to her lips. They already felt badly enough about giving one another up. The last thing she wanted to do was leave him feeling worse than he did already.

Instead, she squeezed his hand and kissed him on the cheek.

She watched as he slowly put his clothes on. The afternoon sun filtered through the blinds, bathing his beautiful body in its glow. She stared at him for the last time and willed the tears not to fall.

He gazed back at her, drinking in the sight of her naked body one last time before leaning down to kiss her once more. "I love you, Letti." Tears welled and ran down his face.

"I love you too, Kevin."

He turned on his heel and left her bedroom.

She didn't move until she heard the front door close. Then with tears pouring down her cheeks, she picked up her underwear and dragged it back on. Her shirt and yoga pants were next.

By then she was crying uncontrollably, heaving sobs tearing through her body. She'd done the right thing. She knew that deep in her soul. It would have been wrong, so wrong to tie him to her when she couldn't fulfill his dream.

But watching him walk out of her door tore the soul from her body.

She let herself cry until there were no more tears to fall. Then she laid down on the bed and breathed in the smell of Kevin and what they'd shared for the last time this afternoon.

Grief enveloped her as she thought about what she had done. For the second time in her life, she'd made the decision to give up her dream. Because, foolishly, she'd begun dreaming of a future with Kevin. Living with him. Marrying him. Acting with him at the Durango. Loving him for the rest of her life.

For the second time, she'd given up her dream because another person's welfare meant more to her than her own.

She'd put Kevin first, the way she'd put Sophie first all those years ago.

Both times she'd done the right thing.

And both times she'd given away a piece of her soul.

Chapter Fourteen

Letti glanced at the clock on the classroom wall. Ten more minutes and class would be over and she could escape to her office for a few minutes before heading over to the Durango. When she'd auditioned for *South Pacific,* she hadn't considered that the last two intense weeks of rehearsals coincided with the start of the first flex semester as well as the continuation of the regular fall semester. Which meant that she would be juggling three balls at the same time: teaching her regular classes, getting her flex students started, and reporting every night to the Durango. Piss-poor planning on her part. If she'd thought ahead, she would have skipped *South Pacific* altogether and picked up with the next production, which would be the holiday show.

Or maybe she would have still been in *South Pacific.*

Maybe it was her broken heart talking today.

She clicked on the next slide in her Power Point presentation. This semester she'd agreed to haul out her old notes and teach a section of the Development of Western Theater. Today they were covering early Greek drama. Most of her students had never heard of Sophocles, Euripides, or Aeschylus, and had no real interest in them.

Normally she could stimulate their interest with her own enthusiasm, but this semester she could give a damn and it showed. Every morning she promised herself she would do better. Her students had paid good money for the course and deserved better than they were getting from her. Yet every day she let them down with a lackluster lecture that had half of them nodding off.

She would do better the next time they met. Honestly.

The bell sounded and her students gathered up their notebooks and laptops and scurried out of the room. It took her longer to pack up than it did her students, but it wasn't too long before she was in her office, sipping a cold drink before heading out to the theater and another night of heartbreak, working with Kevin as the cast and crew put the finishing touches on *South Pacific.*

This week and then the infamous Tech Week, and then they would slide into the Friday, Saturday, Sunday performance cycle, which was easier than the rehearsal schedule, because they had their weeknights free.

Suddenly swamped with fatigue, she put her head in her hands for a few minutes, resting a bit and summoning up the will to go over to the theater and put in another night working with the man she loved, but couldn't claim as her own.

She finished the soda and headed for the parking lot. A wave of September heat hit her in the face. Unbidden, a memory of a cool breeze wafting off the Pacific teased the edges of her mind. Great. She yanked open the car door and tossed her stuff into the passenger seat. Now she had two sets of lost dreams haunting her. Dreams of California, and the life she would never have there, and dreams of Kevin, and the life she'd never share with him.

It was enough to drive her insane.

The parking lot was almost full when she arrived. She spotted Sophie's old Honda and Wade's pickup. Kevin's Mustang was down on the end. She parked as far away from it as she could. Silly. But she didn't want to find herself walking across a dark parking lot with him later. She didn't trust herself not to wrap her arms around him and beg him to take her back.

She missed him that much.

The stage was set up in classroom-like rows for the sitzprobe, the musical rehearsal where the actors sat in rows and went through the musical numbers. This was the first time the actors would rehearse with the orchestra, who could be heard tuning their instruments in the sound booth upstairs.

Sophie sat with Owen and Wade about halfway back. Kevin was already seated in the back row. Common sense would suggest that Letti sit somewhere near him since they sang several songs together, but she wasn't feeling sensible, so she sat down one row from the front.

Rachel was standing at the foot of the stage conferring with the musical director, probably deciding which individual pieces to rehearse first before they ran through the whole thing. Suddenly exhausted, Letti would have loved nothing more than to get in the car and go home to her bed. Her blood sugar was probably low. She reached in her tote bag, grabbed her last candy bar, and settled in for the long rehearsal.

Rachel was in her usual nitpicking mode and the musical director wasn't much better. It was almost ten when they finally called it quits. Letti was in no mood to linger but found herself waylaid by Owen.

"Is it time to start filling out financial aid forms and such?" he asked. "When's the deadline?"

"For most of the private schools it's March. I can look at the applications Sophie's been filling out and get the exact dates. I'll email them to you. Does that work?"

He nodded. "How's the application process coming?"

Letti winced inwardly. The truth was, she didn't know for sure. She'd reminded Sophie several times, and each time Sophie had assured her that she'd been working on them. But Letti hadn't looked at the applications. Between her job, the Durango, and too many hours brooding over what was never going to be with Kevin, she hadn't taken the time to check them. Something she needed to do. But she didn't need to tell Owen all of that.

"Sophie's been working on them since the middle of the summer," she said. "She's applying to quite a few schools, none of which use a common application like the state schools, so it's taking some time."

"Gotcha. If you need anything else from me, let me know."

"Money?" she asked dryly.

"I wish I was making what I did on the force."

"So do I," Letti admitted. "But we'll manage."

Wade put his arm around Owen's shoulders. "You need to quit feeling bad about money. You're doing fine."

They said their good nights. Letti watched wistfully as the two of them walked away. The parking lot was almost deserted and the Mustang was gone. Kevin must not want to be around her any more than she wanted to be around him. If he hurt the way she did, she could understand. The times they'd been forced to interact during rehearsal had nearly done her in. Being so close. Seeing the pain in his eyes. Feeling the tears in hers.

The lights were on in the upstairs bedrooms when she pulled into the driveway. Sophie's car was in its usual spot, and Letti could hear her on the phone. Letti was tired, but Owen's questions had her wondering how far Sophie had gone in filling out her college applications. She'd seen the girl working occasionally at the computer in the man-cave. But not all that often, and not for very long.

Sophie wasn't going to appreciate Letti for checking up on her progress. Too bad. Getting the applications filled out was too important to her daughter's future. If Sophie was ticked at Letti for checking, so be it.

She powered up the year-old desktop and found the folder of downloaded college applications. She opened the one for USC and stared at the application.

It was blank.

She searched for another USC file but found none. That was all right. Maybe Sophie hadn't started with USC. Letti opened the Boston College file and stared in disbelief. It too was blank. Her heart pounding in her throat, she opened file after file. Julliard. California Institute of the Arts. Carnegie Mellon. Purdue. UCLA. Brown. Loyola.

Every damn one of them was blank.

Sophie hadn't filled out any of them.

She looked again in the folder. At the end of the list, she found the Apply Texas application. It was filled out in its entirety. Below it she found a list of special application requirements for Texas A&M, The University of Texas, Rice, Texas Tech, and the University of Houston, all of which had been either partially completed or filled out in its entirety.

Not one of them was known for its drama department.

What. In. The. Hell.

Letti leapt out of the chair, sending is sprawling. "Sophie! Get down here. Now."

Sophie appeared a moment later, looking puzzled. Letti pointed to the computer. "What's the meaning of this? You haven't touched the applications you downloaded months ago. Instead you've been farting around on an ApplyTexas application to five schools that have nothing to offer you. What in the hell are you thinking?"

Sophie lifted her chin. "Those schools have a lot to offer me."

"Their drama departments are crap. They can't offer you one damned thing. If you think you can have the entrée necessary to act with any of the Texas schools, you're off your mind. You need to get into a college that sets you up for an acting a career."

"I'm not going to any of those colleges," Sophie said. "I'm not going to into acting."

"Don't be ridiculous. Of course you are. That's been your dream since you were a little girl."

"*No*," Sophie exploded. "I'm not going to fucking Hollywood and acting. I don't want a career in the industry. And I'm not going to one of those dumb-ass drama schools. I don't *want* to act. That's your dream, not mine." She stopped and took a breath. "I want to build things."

Letti stared at her, aghast. "You want to *build things?* What in the hell is this all about? You want to act. You want to sing and dance. You've been performing since you were five years old. That's what you want to do. It's what you've always wanted to do."

"No, I don't. You think I do, because you want that for me. I don't want to act. I don't want to sing and dance. I want to build bridges, or design robots, or maybe work on electrical systems. I don't want a career performing."

"Don't be ridiculous. You've wanted it since you were a little girl."

"No, *you've* wanted it since I was a little girl. *You've* pushed and *you've* prodded, and *you've* shoved me up on that stage time after time. It was never my choice one way or the other."

"But you love it. I can see it, every time you're up there."

"I love it as a hobby, Mom. Like Wade loves it, or Vivi loves it. I don't love it enough to make it my life's work."

"But—but you're so good at it," Letti protested. "Sophie, you could do it. Why are you giving up now? How can you throw away your future? You could make it out there. You could be a star. I've busted my ass to make damn sure you get a chance at making it big in the industry and you don't even want it? What in the hell are you thinking?"

"I'm thinking you should have gone on and aborted me and had your chance," Sophie said tightly.

"What? No." Letti looked at her daughter in horror. "I would have never done something like that, and you know it."

"Maybe you should have if you wanted to act in LA that badly," Sophie pressed on. "That's all I've heard, all my life. You lost your chance." Sophie's voice rose. "You lost your chance to be a star because you got pregnant with me and had to come home. Which makes it my fault, I guess. Is this how I have to pay you back? Give up on my own dreams and live yours for you?" Sophie fisted tears off her cheeks. "Is that all I am to you? A way to live out your dreams secondhand?"

A harsh sob tore from Sophie's throat, then another, before she turned and ran up the stairs.

Letti stared after her daughter in shock. *Sophie doesn't want it.* She didn't want to sing and dance. She didn't want to act. She didn't want to be a star. She wanted to fucking build things.

Ten long years of hard work wasted.

Ten long years of effort down the drain.

Sophie was going to throw it all away.

Letti slid down on the sofa. Tears ran down her face and dripped on her shirt. If she was any kind of mother, she would go up those stairs and smooth things over with Sophie, assure the girl that her mother loved her and that she was worth much, much more to Letti than the dreams that had been abandoned. But Letti was too hurt, too heartsick. She had thrown herself into making it possible for Sophie to have a chance, to have what Letti had been denied. To live out the dream as Letti hadn't been able to. To learn it meant nothing to Sophie killed.

The girl didn't want it. She wanted something else entirely.

Letti had dreamed for years that Sophie could be a star. She had worked her butt off so Sophie could have her chance, and her daughter had thrown it back in her face.

The last of Letti's dreams was gone.

Now what?

***

Letti fought not to scream in frustration. Honest to god, this had to be the biggest collection of morons she'd ever tried to teach.

"No, I don't think it's legitimate to compare the dialogue in *Dumb and Dumber* to the Greek comedies. The plot of that movie functions to string together a series of gags and does it effectively. But that's all it does. The Greek comedies, on the other hand, frequently satirized the local politicians or communicated politically charged concepts and opinions. Now, can anyone think of a modern comedy that does that?"

The class stared at her. "*The Graduate*? *Network*? *South Pacific*?" she prompted impatiently.

They sat silent for a minute. "I haven't seen any of those," a girl on the front row said.

"They're all old," another piped up.

Letti bit back a sarcastic crack. To this generation, those were old movies. Ancient, even.

"What about *X-Men*?" a young man on the back row asked.

"Well, okay. That one kind of does. Can you think of any others?"

It was like pulling teeth, but the students came up with a few more examples. Her ill temper faded by the end of class, only to be replaced with the funk that seemed to be her constant companion these days.

She was bone tired. Her body insisted she go home and lay down, but it was the Tuesday of tech week and there was no way she could miss tonight's rehearsal. She got a soda and a candy bar from her office refrigerator and made the short drive to the Durango. A quick survey of the parking lot revealed Sophie's car and the all-too-familiar Mustang. Tears stung her eyes as she remembered the late-night ride to the condo at Canyon Lake. It had been four months since she and Kevin had taken that ride to have a fling, which turned out to be so much more.

It felt like a lifetime ago.

She dragged herself to the ladies' dressing room. Sophie was already in the first of her Liat costumes, an Asian-styled high-necked blouse and baggy pants. Her daughter's lips tightened and she turned away. Sophie hadn't said two words to her since their blow-up last week. Letti hadn't said many more to her daughter. There was a yawning gulf between them now, a chasm that neither of them seemed willing or able to breach. Letti had checked the folder of college applications a couple of times, and those to the drama colleges were still blank. She hadn't had the heart to look at the ApplyTexas file.

The thought of that application sitting there ready to go made her want to cry.

She ignored the chatter around her and donned the first of the Bloody Mary costumes. It also consisted of a high-necked Asian blouse and pants, but where Sophie's was designed to make her look beautiful and alluring, the too-baggy pants and shirt of the Bloody Mary outfit went for a comic appearance. Since they weren't rehearsing in makeup tonight, she slapped on the costume's hat and plopped down on a stool to wait for her first scene.

Rachel began the rehearsal promptly. Letti could hear Cameron and Sasha singing "Some Enchanted Evening" in the first scene. Any other time she would have been thrilled by the way their voices blended into a thing of beauty. Tonight it left a bitter taste in her mouth. But any love song would have done that. Still, she was glad the main characters were being acted so well. If her own performance was lackluster, it wouldn't matter as much.

Not that she would do any less than her best. She simply wasn't sure if her best was even going to be up to par tonight.

Her first scene was called. She and Owen slipped into their roles as Luther Billis and Bloody Mary, rivals in the island trinket trade. Then Kevin appeared as Joseph Cable. It wasn't easy, but she stayed in character and delivered the famous "You sexy man" line and tried to sell him a shrunken head. Then she turned to the "island" across the water, an incredibly beautiful set backdrop, and sang "Bali Ha'i," Bloody Mary's tribute to the mystical island the sailors all longed to see. Letti poured her own wistfulness into the song, making it reverberate with deep desire for a mythical place of beauty and joy. The minute the scene was over, she fled to the dressing room, where she mingled with the other women in the cast. She and Sophie continued to ignore one another until Letti's next scene was called.

Rachel called them all together after the last curtain. Letti wondered if her performance was about to be critiqued. Her portrayal of Bloody Mary had been off and she knew it. Between feeling like shit physically, the heartbreak of losing Kevin, and Sophie's devastating announcement, Letti hadn't done half the job she should have. But Rachel's remarks were addressed to everyone and mostly encouraging. If she'd noticed Letti's less than stellar performance, she'd chosen not to mention it.

Letti dragged herself home and went to the kitchen to warm up some leftover spaghetti, took one look at the kitchen and stomped up the stairs. "Damn it, Marco, the kitchen's a mess. Get down there and get it cleaned up. *Now.*"

Marco looked at her with wide eyes. "But I didn't leave it a mess, Mom. I cleaned my stuff up. Sophie warmed her supper after I did."

"Oh. Sorry." Damn. Now she was snapping at Marco for a mess he hadn't even made.

Right now, life was shit, and things did not look like they were going to get any better.

Chapter Fifteen

Letti sat on a kitchen stool and sipped her second cup of Saturday morning coffee. They had managed to survive the dress rehearsal and opening night with only a couple of minor gaffes, and everyone was breathing a bit easier. The newspaper write-ups had all been complimentary. The pressure would be on again next week when the Navarros made their customary visit, but she and the rest of the cast could relax a bit and enjoy putting on their Saturday night and Sunday afternoon shows.

Even after sleeping in, she was still exhausted and had begged off breakfast with her mother and grandmother, who had skipped opening night and were coming the same night as the Navarros. Not too long ago she would have bounced right back after sleeping until ten and been ready to tackle the day. Maybe getting older contributed some, but if she were being honest with herself, which she hated doing, losing Kevin, watching Sophie take a sharp turn into who knows what future, and Letti not having any dreams left to hang on to all played into her feeling like shit.

She finished the coffee and put her cup in the sink. The house was eerily quiet. Sophie and Marco had elected to spend the weekend at Owen and Wade's house, even though it was technically her weekend with them. They probably wanted to get away from her, and she didn't blame them. She wouldn't want to be around herself right now either. If she and Kevin were still dating, they would have gleefully taken advantage of the child-free house and made love all night and half the morning. A tear ran down her face and it was all she could do to not break down crying.

She didn't know if she was ever going to get over him.

She ran upstairs for a shower and was pulling on a ratty pair of cutoffs when the doorbell rang. Swearing under her breath, she threw on a tee and took her time walking down the stairs, hoping that whoever it was would take the hint and go away. But the doorbell

rang again. She peeked out the window and spotted her mother's
Ford in the driveway. She wondered what was going on. It wasn't
like her mother to drive all the way across town if she didn't have to.

She opened the door to find not only her mother but her
grandmother on the front porch. Her mother held out a sack from the
bakery. "We thought since you were too tired to come to us, we
would come to you," her mother said.

Letti's eyes stung with unshed tears. "That was lovely of you.
Come on in."

Her mother handed her the sack and helped *Abuela* maneuver her
walker over the threshold. Letti ushered them to the kitchen table.
"Coffee?"

They both nodded. Letti started a cup and got out silverware. She
put the first cup in front of her grandmother and got out plates while
the second cup brewed. She handed her mother the second cup and
sank into the chair. "Thanks for doing this. I feel terrible not coming
over this morning. But I feel awful. I slept late, and it didn't help."

Her mother looked at her with alarm. "Are you sick, *mija*?"

"No, just tired."

"And unhappy," *Abuela* piped up.

Ya think? "I'm all right, *Abuelita*."

"If you're all right, why did Owen call your mother and say you
needed cheering up? Your children are worried about you. They told
him and he told your mother."

Letti cringed. It wouldn't have taken rocket science for the kids
to see that she wasn't herself. And they knew at least some of the
reason why. Maybe not all, but some.

Her mother passed out the sweetbreads. "No tacos today. The
taco truck was parked somewhere else."

"These are fine." Letti took a bite out of the sweetbread. "And
much appreciated."

They ate in silence for a few minutes. "Do you want to talk about
it?" her mother asked softly.

"I don't know. Are you going to start in again about realistic
goals and dating older men?" Her mother and grandmother looked at
one another. That was exactly what they had planned to say.
"Because if you do, no, I don't want to talk about, and I'm begging
you not to make me listen to the same refrain."

"Okay, then," Mom said. "Let's talk about Sophie. *Mija*, if she wants to go to an engineering school and build things, why shouldn't she?"

"If that's her dream," *Abuela* added.

Letti's eyes narrowed. "This out of the two women who did everything they could to keep me from going off to acting school in California and having a shot at living mine? I wouldn't have gotten to go if Grandma Cheryl hadn't guilted you into it. I would have had to stay right here in town and become a teacher because that's what you wanted for me. So why was it wrong for me to want to live my dreams and okay for Sophie to want to live hers?"

"Because we've grown wiser over the years?" her mother asked quietly. "I hate to say it, *mija*, but aren't you doing the same thing to her that we tried to do to you? Expecting her to live the life you want her to have rather than the one she wants."

Letti's eyes filled. "I thought that *was* what she wanted. I worked for ten damned years so she could have what I couldn't. One careless night and it was all over and I was back here teaching like you wanted me to do all along. I thought if I couldn't have my dream, maybe she could. I dreamed of stardom for her. But no. I have to watch as my last and final dream gets tossed in the trashcan. *Nothing* I've ever dreamed of has come to pass for me. Nothing."

Her mother and grandmother looked at one another. "What else have you dreamed of, *mija*?" *Abuela* asked. "Besides Hollywood?"

Letti wiped her eyes on her napkin. "Never mind. It was a foolish dream. You don't want to hear about it."

"Does it have anything to do with that *muchacho rico* you were seeing for a while?" her grandmother pressed.

Letti swallowed. "It has everything to do with him."

Her mother's eyes flashed. "Did he break up with you, *mija*? I was afraid he would hurt you."

"No, Mom, nothing like that. He loves me as much as I love him."

"You love him?" her mother asked.

"He loves you?" *Abuela* echoed.

"Yes, we love each other. It damned near killed me to let him go."

"Why did you let him go, *mija*? If you love one another?" Her mother laid her hand on Letti's arm.

"He's twenty-five years old. He wants a family. He wants children of his own, and I can't give them to him. Menopause has already started. I haven't had a period in months." She wiped away fresh tears. "I couldn't do that to him. Rob him of his dream. I know how it feels to watch everything you've ever dreamed of go down the drain, and I'll be damned if I do that to him."

"I never thought of that," her mother murmured.

"Letting him go was the right thing. But it hurts. It hurts so damned bad." She looked at her mother and grandmother through her tears. "I did the right thing when I gave up my dream to have Sophie, and I did the right thing by giving up Kevin. I've spent my life doing what's right for everyone around me. When am I ever going to get to do what's right for me? When are any of my dreams for me going to come true?" She put her face in her hands and sobbed.

She felt tender arms go around her shoulders. "*Mija*, I'm sorry. I am so, so sorry," her mother said as she held Letti.

Letti cried for a long time in her mother's arms. She mourned the long-lost dreams of stardom. She cried for Kevin and the life she would never share with him. She cried for the loss of her dreams for Sophie. The tears finally stopped flowing and Letti raised her head, as her mother released her.

"You're a brave woman," her mother said. "Brave and good. Most women would have held on to the young man, whether it was the right thing for him or not. You love him enough to let him go."

"And a lot of girls would have not had their baby. Or dumped *la bebe* on their mother and gone ahead with their plans. You not only had your child, you raised her yourself. You were a *buena madre* to her and to her *hermanito*," *Abuela* added. "That means a lot."

"*Mija*, we *know* you've always done the right thing for everyone," her mother assured her. "It's one of the many things we admire about you and love you for. Your willingness to put others first. To give of yourself to those around you. To do what's best for them, even if it's not what was best for you."

"And you will be blessed for it," *Abuela* added.

"You always said the sadder a woman's life is here, the more blessed she will be in the next one. I wish I believed that," Letti said bitterly.

"Not in the next life. In this one," *Abuela* said. She reached out and gripped Letti's hand. "*Ahora. No luego. Ahora. Pronto.*" Now. Not later. Now. Soon.

Her grandmother believed she would be blessed now. In this life. And it would be sooner rather than later.

"Yes, you gave up your dreams of Hollywood and stardom," her mother said, "but in doing so, you were blessed with the most beautiful, talented, wonderful little girl God ever made. That girl's the light of your life, even if you two are at odds right now over her future. After Sophie, you were blessed with her brother. Another wonderful child. Letti, you were immeasurably blessed for your first sacrifice. *Abuela*'s right. You will be immeasurably blessed for this one as well."

Letti patted her mother's hand. She didn't necessarily believe what her they said, but the thought was sweet and kind.

They ate for a while in silence, then talked of other things until her mother and grandmother left. She watched out the window as they backed out of the driveway. They knew she had made sacrifices for the good of others and admired her for it. They thought she was brave and good. They thought she had been immeasurably blessed for her first sacrifices and would be blessed for this one as well. Her grandmother felt she would be blessed in this life, not the next.

Parents and grandparents lied to the children and grandchildren all the time to make them feel better.

Letti was grateful for their effort.

***

Kevin rubbed his aching neck and sipped his cold coffee. He'd hit the books all day yesterday until he had to go to the theater for the Saturday evening performance, and had been back at it since about eight this morning. His father had warned him that law school was no walk in the park, and he'd been right. Kevin had never had so much thrown at him in so short a period of time. But he was enjoying his studies. Despite the pressure, he found the study of law fascinating, particularly constitutional law. If the rest of law school was as interesting as the first year was shaping up to be, he was going to enjoy it despite the hard work involved.

Which is what Letti had said to him. The more interesting the coursework, the less onerous the learning process.

He shoved that thought from his mind and eyed the clock in the corner of his computer screen. He didn't have to leave for the theater for another hour. He'd skipped breakfast and his stomach was growling and his refrigerator was empty. It wasn't in his nature to mooch, but his mother had made it clear that he was welcome in her kitchen anytime. There would be a refrigerator full of goodies and there might even be someone around to talk to.

Which would beat eating the dregs in his own fridge and thinking about Letti.

He swore out loud and closed down the screen. He didn't know why he kept kidding himself. He was going to think about her whether he was alone or in a crowd. He'd thought about her pretty much twenty-four-seven since he'd walked out of her house six weeks, three days, and twenty-one hours ago. It didn't seem like he was going to quit thinking about her any time in the upcoming decade.

He shut down his laptop and walked out the door. A blast of hot air hit him in the face. It was almost October, but it would be hot for another month and he allowed himself a moment to recall the cool breezes of California in the spring and summer. He loped across the backyard past the pool and shaded patio to his mother's back door.

The kitchen was empty, but he could hear a television upstairs, so somebody had to be home. The refrigerator was stocked with his favorite sandwich fixings, and a loaf of the artisan bread he loved sat on the counter.

Kevin smiled. His mother had shopped with him in mind. She was glad he was home and it showed. He made himself a roast beef sandwich, thought about how long it would be until he could eat again, and made a second. He was headed to the table when his father wandered in, sporting a loose tee and an old pair of jogging shorts. His hair was mussed and he hadn't shaved. Kevin made a production of eyeing him up and down. "Love the look. Have you tried it out in Judge Barrera's courtroom?"

"No, but word has it that Judge Farrell's a sucker for sexy lawyers sporting a three-day growth of beard. Maybe I'll try it there."

"I'll have to remember that someday when I go before her. Where's Mom?"

His dad's face darkened. "She's on her way to Pleasanton to get Emma. Ross is falling-down drunk again and Emma wanted out of there." He took a deep breath. "Another month and she can move here if she wants to."

"She'll want to. Can I make you a sandwich?"

"Don't mind if you do. Turkey for me instead of the roast beef, though."

Kevin made his father a sandwich. They carried their sandwiches, along with a bag of potato chips and sodas, to the table in the air-conditioned sunroom. "We've both been so busy I've barely spoken two words to you," his father commented. "How are you liking law school?"

"Utterly fascinating," Kevin said between bites.

"What do you like best so far?"

"Constitutional law, of all things. The way the constitution dictates and influences the parameters of our government. Almost makes me want to go into politics."

"Exactly what this country needs. Another lawyer running for office." Dad rolled his eyes.

"Sorry about that. But lots of lawyers are involved in politics. Yourself included. I remember all the meetings you used to go to, and all the behind the scenes work you used to do."

"I was tempted to run for office too, when I was your age. Glad you're liking law school. Good."

"I am. I'm almost sorry I didn't go straight from college."

"Nah, you needed to get the *I'm going to be a famous actor* thing out of your system. Otherwise, you'd have always wondered about the road not taken. This way, you know you're doing the right thing."

"That's kind of what happened with Letti. She never got her chance in LA and she's spent her entire life wishing she had and regretting the fact that she didn't."

"Really? How is Letti?" His father eyed him shrewdly.

Uh-oh. His father was fishing.

He may as well be honest. His father was going to find out anyway. "I haven't heard from her, so I can't say I know for sure how she is these days. But I heard via the grapevine that she had a major blow-up with her daughter over where Sophie's going to go to college. Letti's hot for Sophie to go to a performing school so she can go to LA and act, and Sophie wants to go to engineering school so she can build things. I do know Letti's been off her game on the stage for the last couple of weeks. She's not turning in anywhere near the performance she's capable of."

"I see." His father paused a minute. "A lot of your scenes are with her. Are you turning in the performance you should be?"

He ran his hand down the side of his cheek. "Probably not. You can see for yourself next Saturday. I understand the Navarros are taking you out to dinner before the show."

"The corporation opened a new fusion restaurant in the Pearl District. Ernest and Clarissa want to show it off. Your mother's looking forward to it."

"I'm sure."

"So, if you don't mind my asking, did something happen between you and Letti? The last I heard it was still hot and heavy between the two of you."

"It's not anymore." Kevin's stomach clenched. "We called it off a while back. I didn't want to break things off but she insisted."

"I was afraid it was something like that, the way you've been moping when you think your mother and I aren't looking. Sometimes that happens. The fling is over before you want it to end."

"It was more than a fling, Dad. We fell in love." He took a breath. "I've had some girlfriends along the way, and I've had what you'd call a fling or two, but I've never felt anything like this for any of them. I've never loved anyone the way I love her."

His father eyed him thoughtfully. "You said you both fell in love. Did she love you the way you love her?"

"In all honesty, probably more. She's older, knows what the hell love is all about and I have no doubt she loves me."

"So what gives?"

"You know I've always wanted a family. Ever since Emma was born, I've wanted a family of my own."

"It started a long time before Emma. Do you remember that baby doll you had when you were little?"

"I had a baby doll?"

"Yep. You had a little boy doll. You named him 'Boy Baby' and you took him everywhere. You loved that doll. I even started wondering if you were gay, which goes to show how much I knew about little boys back then. You moved on to other toys when you started school, but your mother and I surmised, correctly, it seems, that it was a portent of things to come. Your mother rescued that doll out of your closet and stored it with her most precious keepsakes." He looked at Kevin with love and discernment. "You still want that family."

"Letti can't give me that family," Kevin said, cursing the tears that threatened. "She's already started menopause. The women in her family get it early. She saw me with Vivi Abonce's baby and then we ran into Jessica Clary and her fiancé and they're already pregnant. Letti could tell how badly I want that. She said we needed to break it off before we're in so deep that breaking it off would be worse than doing it now. But you know, I don't think it could hurt much more than it does. I love her. I don't know how I fell for her so damned fast, but I did. I left a huge piece of myself behind when I walked out of her house that afternoon." He turned to his father. "A piece of myself I don't think I can ever get back. I want that family, Dad. But I love her, and I want her. Now I can't imagine having a family with anyone else but her."

"What did she say about that? Did she tell you she was through raising children?"

"Quite the opposite. She told me she'd have my babies in a heartbeat if she could. It's not that she doesn't want more children. Her body's shutting down."

"I see."

Kevin braced himself for his father to dismiss his concerns and tell him he'd get over Letti. Instead, Dad looked at him thoughtfully. "Did the two of you talk this out, or did you make an impulsive decision to separate?"

"It was quick. One minute we were together and the next minute we weren't."

"I see. Are you regretting that impulsive decision?"

"Every minute of every day."

A small smile touched his father's lips. "Kind of reminds me of when your mother and I were busy falling in love and faced with some hard choices. We too made an impulsive decision that almost cost us our relationship."

"Oh?" Kevin's head popped up. "What impulsive decision?"

"I believe I mentioned earlier that at one time I was tempted to run for office. It was a lot more than me being tempted. I dreamed about it from the time I was eight years old, when I watched the Kennedy-Nixon debates on television and Kennedy's inauguration. I was going to be the next John F. Kennedy. I volunteered in the sixty-eight and seventy-two presidential elections, and a couple of congressional elections as well. I was making a name for myself behind the scenes, and they were grooming me to run for City Council a few years down the line. Then I met Barbara Beasley. The most perfect girl in the world. Until she opened her mouth."

"The stutter."

"The stutter. Your mother was horribly self-conscious about stuttering."

"She still is. She hates talking in front of people she doesn't know. Which as a politician's wife she would be expected to do often and well."

"The thought positively paralyzed her. We promised ourselves we wouldn't get serious and then did it anyway. We fell in love. At that point my plans to run for office became a bone of contention. We argued about it. She told me she wasn't going to stand in the way of something I'd wanted all my life and gave me my walking papers." His father's expression turned distant. "Except for watching them lower your sister into the ground, that has to be the most painful moment of my life. To see your mother get in her old Chevy Nova and drive off." His father fell silent.

"What happened next?"

"I put in the loneliest three months you can imagine. I was miserable. And I did a lot of hard thinking. Our decision to separate had been made on the spur of the moment, without us doing any real thinking about our decision. I began to wonder if we should have thought it through more thoroughly before we pulled the trigger. I contemplated two futures. One in the public eye with a woman I might not love at my side. Or a future out of the spotlight with the girl of my dreams."

"You chose Mom and gave up politics."

"I didn't give up politics. I gave up running for office, which is a big difference. I got my political fix by continuing to work behind the scenes, and I've never regretted it. In all fairness, it wasn't an easy decision to make because I would be sacrificing something I'd always dreamed of. But my point is that you and Letti did the same thing. You gave up one another without thinking things through. And now you at least regret that. Does she?"

"I don't know. Letti and I haven't exchanged two words since. I can see the hurt in her eyes when she looks at me. Which makes me think she misses me as much as I miss her."

"Okay. Listen Kevin, loving someone sometimes means making some hard choices. That's what you're looking at here. A life with the family you've always wanted, or life with the woman you love. Not an easy call. Much harder than the one your mother and I had to make. I get that. One you need to think long and hard about."

"I've done nothing but think about it for the last six weeks," Kevin admitted. "And I'm no closer to an answer than I was the afternoon I walked away from Letti. I love her so much. But I want a family. You and Mom deserve more grandchildren."

"Your mother and I are the last thing you need to be worried about. This is your decision. You and the woman you love should be your only consideration. The only thing I can tell you for sure is that you and your lady needed to do a lot more thinking before you made that kind of monumental decision. It's not too late to reverse that decision if it was the wrong one." A small smile played around his lips. "And it might not be a matter of either-or. Maybe you and Letti need to start thinking a bit more creatively. Outside the box. If she's genuinely ready to raise another family with you, there are options. Now that I've said my piece, I need to take a shower before your mother and Emma get here. And I do believe you have a play to put on." Dad picked up their empty plates and disappeared into the house.

Hmm. Now he had to think about what his father meant by creative and options.

Chapter Sixteen

Letti sat at the dining room table with a stack of pop quizzes in front of her. The Dilberts in her Development of Western Theater class had been paying attention after all. Most of them were getting at least some of the answers right. Considering her flagging energy level by the time of day the course rolled around, she was amazed they were paying any attention whatsoever to her lackluster delivery.

The next unit covered ancient Roman theater, about which less was known than Greek. Letti didn't plan to spend a great deal of time on that era. Students were typically more interested in Medieval and Renaissance period theater, out of which modern theater evolved. That was understandable. She found it more interesting as well, and hoped by the time she got to that point in the course she felt like teaching the material with the enthusiasm her students deserved. It didn't help that she had five more weeks of *South Pacific* to get through where she had to face the man she loved and could never have. She couldn't wait to not have to deal with that. Seeing Kevin was dragging her down more than anything else.

The front door flew open and Sophie barreled inside, coming to a halt when she spotted Letti at the dining table. "Dad's gonna call you," she said tightly as she headed for the stairs.

"Whatever," Letti murmured under her breath.

She started to ask where Sophie had been but remembered something about a Tuesday evening engineering club meeting. She and Sophie were still barely speaking. Letti had yet to resign herself to Sophie's career choice and she showed no sign of changing her mind.

Letti's mother had been right. Letti was guilty of doing the exact same thing to Sophie that they had done to her. But Sophie had so damn much acting talent. It was a crime to waste that talent on the community theater stage, even one as distinguished as the Durango.

Sophie was meant for greater things.

Letti finished the last quiz in the stack and was returning them to her briefcase when Owen's name appeared on her telephone screen. "Sophie said you'd be calling," she said without preamble.

"She's asked me to take over the college search. I said I'd do it if you were okay with it."

"Knock yourself out," Letti said tiredly. "She's probably afraid I'll delete the ApplyTexas and fill out the others."

"You wouldn't do that to her. Would you?"

"I wouldn't do that," she said tiredly. She'd been tempted, though.

"I'll be there in a few minutes. Can you email me the ApplyTexas application and gather up whatever papers you have?"

"Yeah, sure." She emailed Owen the requested items. She loaded the material on a thumb drive as a backup and was gathering up the paper forms when the doorbell rang. Sophie beat her to the door and gave her father a huge hug. "Thanks, Daddy." She beamed at her father. "I appreciate the help."

"It's nothing, princess. Now run on upstairs while I talk to your mother."

Sophie turned to Wade. "And thank you as well. For all the information on engineering schools."

"Glad to help."

Letti gave Wade a look that had him looking sheepish.

Sophie scampered upstairs and Letti gestured for Wade and Owen to come in. "I emailed the ApplyTexas form, and all her essays and such she wrote for the individual schools. I loaded it all on this thumb drive as well. I didn't bother to load or send the acting schools' applications since she's refusing to fill them out. If by some miracle she changes her mind, let me know." She felt tears threaten and she willed them away. "I think this is everything." Her eyes filled. Damn it all, she was going to break down and cry in front of Owen and Wade. She thrust the stack toward Owen. "Here. Take it."

Owen took the stack of papers. She slid down on the sofa and put her face in her hands, unable to stem the river of tears that sprang to her eyes. She felt the couch seat depress next to her. "Letti, talk to me." Owen. He was sitting beside her. "What's got you so tied up in knots that you can't hand me a stack of papers without crying?" He threaded her fingers in his.

Her head snapped up. "You know damned well why I'm tied up in knots. Or you would if you thought about it," she said bitterly.

"Sophie said you were still mad at her for not wanting to go to acting school. But I thought you were angry she wouldn't fill out the applications. I didn't realize you were upset enough to be crying about it. Are you that damned disappointed?"

"Of course, I'm that damned disappointed. Disappointed and heartsick."

"But why?" Wade was mystified and not hiding it. "Engineering's a great career. I love it."

"That's fine for you. But Sophie...Sophie has the potential to be a star, and she's throwing it away like it doesn't matter," Letti protested. "She could've made it out there." Letti knuckled away tears. "She could have had it all. She could have had what I didn't. And now it's all over. None of my dreams will ever come true. Not that one or any of the others."

"What dreams, Letti?" Owen asked quietly.

"Every dream I ever had," she said softly. "A part of me knows I should be grateful for what I have. But those dreams were important to me. And they're not gonna happen. It will never happen for me, and Sophie's turning her back on something few people have. Innate talent."

She looked down at her and Owen's linked hands. "I know it's too late for me. It has been for a while, now. Even if I could wave a magic wand and find myself in LA, I'm past it. I'm too old. So I figured if I couldn't have it, my daughter could. But she's turning it down without giving it a second thought." She took a breath. "I haven't been fair to Sophie. I get that. I know her having that career wouldn't be the same as if it had been me, but it would at least have been something."

Owen looked at her knowingly. "You wouldn't be this upset if it was only the business with Sophie. What other dreams have you lost?"

Fresh tears ran down her face. "Kevin. That dream went up in smoke as well." She pushed herself up from the sofa. "It kills me. Two things. I wanted them both with all my heart. I wanted to act and live in California. Then I wanted to have a life with Kevin. Turns out I can't have that either."

"Did the pissant let you fall in love with him and then dump you?" Wade asked. "Do I need to have a talk with him?"

"No, nothing like that. He loves me as much as I love him."

"So what's the problem? If you're worried about what people are going to think, don't be," Owen said. "Wade and I have rattled more cages than you and Kevin ever would."

"We couldn't care less what the world thinks. The issue is a family. He wants children and I can't give them to him."

"Like mother, like daughter?"

Letti nodded.

Owen turned to Wade. "The women in her family start menopause like ten years earlier than most women."

"That sucks." Wade looked at her with compassion. "I'm sorry, Letti."

"I am too. It breaks my heart. We talked and I told him it wasn't fair to let our relationship cost him everything he ever wanted in this life. It happened to me and I know how it feels."

Owen looked at her thoughtfully. "So you feel everything you ever wanted is down the drain. Your acting career and Kevin."

"Pretty much."

Owen looked at her for a moment. "That is the biggest bunch of bullshit that's ever come out of your mouth," he said, his expression filled with exasperation.

"What?" Letti leapt off the sofa. She planted herself in front of him with her hands on her hips. "What the hell kind of thing is that to say? I sat here and poured my heart out to you and you call it bullshit? What kind of jackass are you?"

"The kind who tells you the truth. At least I'm not yelling at you the way you did me a few months ago," Owen continued calmly. "Letti, you're not too damned old for anything you want if you'll reach out and grab it. Every dream you ever had for yourself can come true."

"Yeah, right. Tell that to an industry that thinks women over thirty are past it," she said bitterly. "Tell that to Kevin who wants babies I can't give him anymore."

"Letti, sit down here beside me and think." He patted the sofa beside him. Reluctantly she sat. "Let's talk about LA and this dream that supposedly got away.

"I want you to remember back when we were dating, our junior and senior years at USC. You didn't care about 'the industry.' You didn't care where you acted. You didn't even care what part you played. You would get up on a stage anywhere they'd let you. Even though you could have, you didn't spend your summer in Los Angeles acting on those stages. We went to Noplace, Mississippi and worked at one of those dinner playhouses that were still around back then. You had the time of your life on that Mississippi stage. It wasn't making it big you dreamed of back then. It was acting itself. Do you remember? We even laughed about it. LA or Mississippi. It was all the same to us."

She looked at him balefully. "That's because I thought I'd have it someday."

"That may be so. But that wasn't your motivation, while we were in school or later when we first came back here. You were perfectly happy on the local stages. The Durango, the Playhouse, the community theaters in Boerne and New Braunfels. You didn't give a damn what stage you were on. You wanted to be on one, and that's all that mattered." He swallowed. "It was only when our marriage started to go sour that being in LA became the greatest dream you'd never have. It was only after the divorce that it became your be-all and end-all."

"And you think this because?" she asked tightly.

"I was married to you for nearly fifteen years. I know you mighty well, Letti. I watched you change. And it broke my heart because I knew I was mostly to blame."

"There's no point in assigning blame. It's water under the bridge," she said.

"Really? Letti, you need to ask yourself what your dream really was back then and what it could be now. What's more important to you? What's going to make you happy? Being a 'star' in Tinseltown, or acting, period? Twenty years ago, you would've said acting was more important. Maybe that needs to become your passion again. Not LA, but acting and doing it well. Entertaining the people of your hometown. Bringing them a level of excellence they wouldn't get otherwise.

He shook his head. "There are theaters all over the region that would love to cast you in their productions. There are plenty of roles that cry out for a talented forty-year-old. Roles you can sink your teeth into." He grabbed her hand again and squeezed. "Your dream is right in front of you. It's got your name on it. All you have to do is reach out and take it."

He paused and took a deep breath. "A few months ago, you as much as told me the same thing. To reach out and claim the man I love. I'm telling you what I know is true, only I'm telling you to reach out for the acting you love so much. It's yours if you want it."

Wade sat down on the other side of her. "Maybe you need to think again about Kevin too. He's been so down lately. He loves you, Letti. I can see it every time he lays eyes on you. Reach out for that dream as well."

"It wouldn't be fair to him. To reach out and claim my dream at the expense of his."

"What makes them mutually exclusive? Are you willing to raise a family with him?"

"I would if I could. But I can't make those babies he wants so much."

"Who says you have to make them?" Wade pushed.

"Who the hell else is gonna make them?"

Wade rolled his eyes. "There's a world out there full of children who don't have a family. You and Kevin could give a couple of them a home."

"Kevin wants his own kids. I doubt with their money and their social status that any of the Summersets are going to be open to adoption," Letti stated.

Wade raised his eyebrow. "Thank god the Rileys don't feel that way."

Letti felt her face redden. "Oh, I'm so sorry. I forget you're adopted. I'm such an ass."

Wade leaned forward. "You just made my point better than I could have. You're supposed to forget kids are adopted. You and Kevin would love your children dearly, and honey, you'll never think of them as adopted. My mom has four kids she loves with all her heart, and she didn't give birth to a one of us."

"If Kevin is bound and determined the swimmer has to be his, there's such a thing as technology. And surrogacy. There are all kinds of ways to become parents these days. With the kind of money those people have, you could take that route," Owen suggested.

"Please give it some thought," Wade said. "All of your dreams can come true, Letti. None of it's out of your reach. Think about it. Please."

***

Kevin parked his car and dragged himself to the back door of the theater. A warm breeze lifted the hair at his temples. He spotted Wade and Owen striding across the parking lot and waited for them to join him. "Well, are you ready?" Wade asked, his eyes snapping.

"You mean am I prepared to put on the performance of a lifetime for the Navarros? Absolutely. Although I'm not sure why everybody's so wound up about them. They're nice people."

"Never said they weren't," Owen said. "But their contributions are a major part of what's keeping this place up and running, and they expect only the best. Not that your folks haven't been wonderful and generous in the extreme. But..." Owen lifted his hands.

"But *El Jefe* and Mrs. Navarro's contributions are an order of magnitude greater. I get that. Mom and Dad joke about how rich the Navarros are."

"So do Gramps and Gran Riley," Wade said. "Are you ready to wow them?"

"I am," Kevin said. "Them and my parents. Mom and Dad are here tonight."

"I'm ready, too," Owen said. "Although the Navarros might be easier to wow than Letti's mother and grandmother. Sophie said they were bringing Marco tonight."

"Owen, you could earn an Academy Award out there tonight and you couldn't please those two," Wade teased. He turned to Kevin. "He has a permanent spot on their shit list. And I'm right up there beside him."

"I wouldn't worry about it," Owen laughed. "They're here for Letti and Sophie, not me. And we're all going to have to really up our game if we want to best Letti's performance last night." His whistled under his breath. "I've acted with her for twenty-plus years and I've never seen her put on a show like she did last night. I've never been prouder of her."

"Yeah, she gave the rest of us something to live up to, didn't she?" Wade said thoughtfully. He started to say more, but Owen caught his eye and shook his head.

Kevin wondered what that was all about as he followed them into the theater.

They were a hundred percent right. Letti's performance last night had been beyond spectacular. It was like a switch had gone on. She'd done a good job during rehearsal, at least until they'd parted ways. She'd risen to the occasion and then some once they were performing in front of an audience. But nothing like last night. There were no words for the performance she'd put on. It was like Letti disappeared and Bloody Mary came to life. Wily, smart, determined, a passionately loving mother driven to obtain the best for her daughter by any means possible. Bloody Mary reached out and grabbed the audience by their hearts, and when Letti came out to take her bows, they surged to their feet and whistled and stomped for a good five minutes. Letti's enthusiasm was catching. Sophie's portrayal of Liat was over-the-top wonderful. He had been affected by the caliber of her performance. Joseph Cable came to life like he hadn't quite before.

Rachel had been smiling like a fool.

He didn't know what had triggered the change in Letti. But whatever happened, he hoped it would still be "on" this evening.

The men's dressing room filled up. He shucked his jeans and tee and donned the World War II style Marine uniform. He and Wade shared a mirror while Owen sat at the next one and applied the special makeup that disguised the scars marring his face. "That stuff's magic," Kevin commented as Owen's scars disappeared.

"That's why Mom calls it 'Angie's Magic,'" Wade said. "Hand me that blush, will you?"

Kevin handed Wade a tube of tan blush and finished his own makeup.

Letti was over in the ladies' dressing room and was probably doing the same. She didn't need to change her skin tone, but she and Sophie both applied liner and shadow around their eyes to make them look more Vietnamese. Merely the thought of her made his midsection tighten and his cock jerk. His mind drifted to the morning he'd leaned against her bathroom door and watched her apply her makeup. It had been a turn-on watching her go from naturally beautiful to sophisticated and glamorous. Oddly, that morning was one of his fondest memories of their time together.

An everyday thing. The kind of stuff you get to do with the person you're living your life with. One of the many small intimacies you get to enjoy and share.

One he'd love to repeat over and over.

He finished with his makeup and sat on a stool. The buzz in the dressing room was loud, and the excitement almost palpable. But his thoughts weren't on the performance ahead. He would do well, especially if Letti's Bloody Mary was on fire again. The rest of the cast would also. Instead, he was again thinking about the talk he and his father had shared on the patio. He'd thought about little else this week. About a family. About Letti. About the life they could have together.

About thinking outside the box.

He and Letti needed to talk again. His father was right. They had pulled the plug on their relationship way too soon. Letti had decided that continuing their relationship wouldn't be fair to him. He'd been swayed by her argument and gone along with it. They hadn't discussed it in depth. Neither of them had fought for their relationship the way they should have. He'd bowed to her self-sacrificing, but likely made an erroneous decision. He should have fought. He should have argued.

If they put their relationship back together, he would have to remember that she might be older, but it didn't always make her wiser. He would have to make his feelings known. He would have an equal voice in their decisions and not bow to her supposedly superior wisdom.

A small smile touched his lips. She wasn't always going to like that, but the thought of fighting with her made him harder. He'd take all her passion, any way she had to give it.

They'd both been guilty of not thinking outside the box about his desire for a family. His father had said their future wasn't necessarily an either/or proposition. He'd suggested they think outside the box. Maybe they could find a way to eat their cake and have it too, so to speak.

Dad hadn't come out and said it, but he'd hinted that it was time to think of perhaps another way they could become parents together. But they wouldn't know if any of these possibilities were the answer for them if they continued to avoid one another. They needed to talk. They needed to do it soon.

Like maybe tonight after the show.

The crew chief called the ten-minute warning. He didn't know if he could catch her before the curtain went up. But he could try. He made his way behind the maze of sets and curtains and peeked inside the women's dressing room, where he was treated to the sight of a couple of the ensemble throwing on their World War II style shorts and halters. But no Letti. Nor was she standing in the wings.

He was about to go back to the men's dressing room and wait for his first scene when he spotted her coming out of the unisex restroom looking pale under her makeup. He rushed to her side. "Are you all right?"

She stopped and took a deep breath. "I feel like shit. I must be coming down with something." She smiled faintly. "Don't worry. I'm still getting up there this evening and doing the Durango proud."

"I have no doubt of that." He leaned down, the scent of her shampoo and soap making his heart thump. "Letti, we need to talk. Please." His eyes pleaded with her to say yes.

Her mouth parted slightly in surprise and he felt his face fall. She was going to turn him down. Ah, no. She was going to hear him out, if not tonight then tomorrow or the day after that. They meant too much to one another to throw everything away.

She looked at him and slowly nodded her head. "Okay."

"Tonight?"

"Tonight's as good as any. Pick up some tacos and come by the house."

"Do I bring enough for the kids?"

She shook her head. "The kids are at Owen's again."

Perfect. That was just as well. What he had to say to Letti was for her ears alone.

Letti squeezed his arm and walked away.

Wow. That had been easy.

Unless she was planning to turn him down again. She was going to be in for a shock if she did. He was going to fight her this time. He was going to argue his case. He was going to change her mind about them.

The stage manager called five minutes and they all took their places. Kevin took a breath and prepared to turn into Joseph Cable.

He and Letti would talk tonight. They would find a way to share their lives. They would find a way to be together. They would find a way to have a life that would be happy and fulfilling to them both.

But first he had a performance to give.

Chapter Seventeen

Of course, she'd told him yes. She had been on the verge of calling and asking to talk to him.

Letti trudged back to the ladies' dressing room and flopped down on a stool to wait for her first scene. Spots swam before her eyes and she shut them tightly. Of all nights to feel like shit. With the Navarros out in the audience expecting only the best. There were donors out there besides the Navarros, Kevin's parents among them. Others in the audience who also deserved a great performance, like her mother, grandmother, and Marco. Hell, every patron out there had paid for a ticket and deserved an evening of top-notch entertainment.

She would give them that if it killed her.

She leaned back against the counter. The sound was muffled, but they could still hear Josh welcome the audience and a local radio DJ make a pitch for contributions to a women's shelter. The prelude began and she took a deep breath, and then another. She could do this. She would power through. She wouldn't let her castmates down.

She felt a familiar hand on her shoulder. "You okay, Mom?" Sophie looked at her with concern.

Letti nodded. "I should've eaten a bigger supper."

Sophie dug into her bag and handed Letti a Power Bar. "Maybe this will help."

Letti thanked her and ripped open the wrapper. She and Sophie had reached something of an understanding. Letti gave her blessing to Sophie to go to engineering school if that was what she wanted, but assured her that if she changed her mind, she could apply to the drama schools later on.

Letti still believed that Sophie was making a mistake, but it was Sophie's mistake to make. Further objection to Sophie's decision would not be fair to her precious daughter. It would be pointless as well.

She hoped Sophie would be as talented an engineer as she would have been an actress.

Letti would not be passing the acting torch on to her daughter.

Apparently it was up to her to be the actress in the family.

She stifled a sigh and munched the Power Bar. She felt like absolute shit, but she was still pumped beyond belief for her upcoming performance. She'd tasted delicious anticipation all day. No, all week. Ever since the discussion with Owen.

They might be divorced, but he still understood her, maybe better than she did herself. His observations had been spot on. In the early days, acting itself was her only passion. Her desire to attend USC had been strictly to attend their drama school. She had fallen in love with California once she'd gotten there, but in the beginning making it big had not been her motivation.

Her motivation had been a desire to perform.

Their summer in Mississippi had been proof of that.

Her early years at the Durango and the other local theaters had also been proof. It was only later, as the possibility of her ever returning to California became more and more remote, that the glitz and glamour had become a siren's song. It would always be a lovely daydream, making her living as an actress and working on a studio soundstage or at an on-location shoot. But a daydream was just that. A daydream. A way to pass a few minutes. Not a life's goal. Not something to aspire to. Not a dream to reach for.

Her dream was, and always had been, acting. What she'd wanted all those years ago was to act. What she still wanted to do was act. Any role she could land. Any theater that would cast her. She would spend the rest of her life doing what she loved and sharing her talent with anyone who wanted to watch. Like the Navarros tonight. They'd come to see a quality production. They'd come to see talented acting, superb music, and singing. She would give them what they'd come to see. They would get from her the best performance Letti could give.

Bloody Mary would come to life for them.

But she sure wished she felt better.

Her scene was called and a sudden burst of adrenaline flooded her veins. She took her place on the stage and shut her eyes, letting the character of Bloody Mary take over as she and Owen's Luther Billis argued over who had the best trinkets for sale. Then Kevin's Joseph Cable made his appearance and the wily Bloody Mary sized him up. She and Kevin sang the haunting "Bali Ha'i," their voices reverberating through the theater. The audience sat silent for a beat before breaking into thunderous applause.

Bloody Mary was off to a good start.

Her adrenaline rush suddenly over, she returned to the dressing room and listened to Sasha and Cameron's next scene and the famous "I'm Gonna Wash that Man Right out of my Hair." Then Billis and Cable make their famous visit to Bali Ha'i.

Again Letti became Bloody Mary as she tempted Cable with her beautiful daughter and Cable fell in love with the much younger Liat. Letti managed to stay in character until the scene was finished and then fled to the dressing room and collapsed onto a stool rather than stay in the wings and watch the pivotal scene when Nellie finds out about Emile's native children.

She ate another Power Bar and drank a sugar-laden soda during intermission. Her next scene was perhaps her most important. Her rendition of "Happy Talk" was anything but happy as she tried to get Joseph Cable to imagine life with Liat. She made Bloody Mary's sorrow palpable when, despite Cable's love for Liat, he lets the Tonkinese girl go.

She let the character's deep disappointment in her thwarted plans and Joseph Cable's prejudice shine through, delivering the perfect amount of a mother's contempt in the famous "You stingy bastard" line. She then sank down on a stool in the wings and listened to the famous exchange between Emile and Joseph in which Joseph explains racial prejudice in the song "You've Got to be Carefully Taught," and Emile laments his loss in "This Nearly was Mine."

Her job for the night mostly done, she returned to the dressing room and listened with half an ear to the rest of the production. She felt so bad she almost wished she'd told Kevin to wait until tomorrow to come over. But she hated to make him wait. She suspected that he too had been thinking about their relationship and was having second thoughts about their breakup.

She knew he missed her. Wade was right. It was on Kevin's face every time he looked at her. Besides, she had been ready to call him anyway, to sit down with him and see if there was any way they could cobble together a future that would give them both what they wanted most. She wasn't sure they could do that. Even if they worked out something regarding the family he wanted, they were still fifteen years apart, with all the issues that age gap entailed. Some of those issues might be harder to overcome than that of a family. But they owed it to themselves to try.

She wanted to hear what he had to say. She wanted to hear it tonight.

The muffled sounds of the last few scenes, the gunfire and the radio transmissions, came through the wall. She and Sophie returned for the brief vignette in which they learn that Joseph Cable has been killed, and retreated again for Emile and Nellie's emotional reunion.

The music swelled and the curtain closed on the last scene, and opened again to the thunderous applause of the appreciative audience. Letti loved the sound. It meant the patrons had enjoyed a fine performance. She knew in her heart she had delivered one tonight. Despite feeling terrible, she had delivered a Bloody Mary of which she could be proud.

The nurses and sailors in the ensemble took their bows. Then the minor characters. Then it was her and Owen's turn. He bowed first to a burst of applause, but the audience came apart when she curtsied. They stood and stomped and whistled for a good five minutes, the cast joining in. Her face flushed, she stepped with Owen to one side as Kevin and Sophie came out to bow. Both received a rousing hand, Kevin in particular. Cameron and Sasha also received long, enthusiastic accolades, and she and Sophie and Sasha were handed bouquets of red roses.

The applause finally died down and the cast trooped up a side aisle and lined up in the lobby. Letti found herself standing between Wade and Kevin, with Sophie and Owen nearby. She was acutely conscious of Kevin's presence beside her. But that was superseded by the fatigue that swamped her now that the play was over. She stood up straight and stiffened her back. *Just a few more minutes.* A few minutes of shaking hands and thanking their audience, and she could go home and sit down and eat a taco and hear what Kevin had to say.

If she could stay awake that long.

The entire audience wanted to shake hands. She was surprised to be greeted by several of her students from her afternoon class who asked if the musical was covered in the course. Her mother and grandmother came through the line, generous in their praise to her and Sophie, and even sparing a kind word for Owen and Wade. Marco gave her a hug and fist-bumped his father, sister, and Wade. The Summersets were next. Barbara was, as always, unfailingly gracious. There was speculation in Byron's eyes as he greeted her. It made her wonder how much Kevin had told his father about what had happened.

She shook a few more hands. Then there was a bit of a break. Rachel and development director Maggie Gutierrez were personally escorting Ernest and Clarissa Navarro down the line of actors, introducing cast one by one. The Navarros were taking their time, speaking a bit to each cast member. The way the cast members were beaming, the Navarros must have been saying some lovely things about the performance.

They stopped to speak to Sophie. "You, of course, are going to perform professionally someday," Clarissa said. "You have such talent."

Letti beamed. *Go, Clarissa.*

Owen turned her direction and winked.

"Actually, Mrs. Navarro, I'm going to be an engineer," Sophie said. "But thank you so much for thinking I'm that good."

They then turned to Owen. "I'm glad to see you up there again," *El Jefe* said. "You did an outstanding job in the spring show as well as tonight. It took courage to do Jud Fry without the makeup." Owen thanked them graciously.

They stopped for a moment and shook hands with Kevin. Clarissa beamed. "Barbara and Byron's boy, right? Are you sure you want to be a lawyer? You have such talent on the stage," she gushed.

"Which Byron says will be as useful in the courtroom as it is here, *querida*," *El Jefe* boomed. "We enjoyed your performance tonight. Very much."

Then the power couple moved to Letti and Rachel introduced her and explained that she was Sophie's mother. *El Jefe* looked at her. "Where do I know you from?"

"We've met one other time. I directed *Oklahoma!.*"

"That's right. Well, you were marvelous tonight. Absolutely marvelous," *El Jefe* said.

"Oh, yes. I've never seen Bloody Mary come to life like that. Not even in the movie," Clarissa added.

She was better than Juanita Hall of Broadway and cinema fame? High praise indeed. "Thank you so much."

"I'd like to see you up on that stage again," *El Jefe* continued. "And soon."

"Why, thank you, Mr. Navarro. I'm sure you will."

El Jefe turned to Clarissa. "Wouldn't she be a wonderful Dolly Levi? I would love to see her play that role." He turned to Rachel. "How about it? Can you put *Hello, Dolly!* in the schedule somewhere?"

Rachel's lips twitched and she nodded. "I'll bet that can be arranged sometime in the next year or two."

"Wonderful. I look forward to it."

The Navarros moved on. Letti couldn't contain her smile. The Navarros had enjoyed her performance. They wanted to see her play Dolly Levi. The thought made her positively giddy. Letti had no doubt that Rachel was mentally rearranging next year's lineup, figuring out where to insert *Hello, Dolly!* into the next season. If they wanted to see her play Dolly Levi, she would give them the Dolly Levi of a lifetime.

She felt herself grow lightheaded from the praise. Or maybe it wasn't from the praise. Spots danced before her eyes and her knees grew weak. She reached out and clutched Kevin's arm. "Kevin, I—"

She felt his arms go around her as she sank.

***

Kevin tightened his arms around Letti as she fell. *Oh, my God.* She'd said she didn't feel well tonight. She shouldn't have gone on. She should be home in bed. The Navarros could have come another night.

She'd taken "the show must go on" a little too far.

She was scaring the shit out of him.

He looked toward Sophie and Owen. "Somebody call an ambulance," he called out in panic. "Wade, help me." Wade took hold of Letti's other arm. "Somebody call nine-one-one, please."

Owen shook his head. "Not necessary. Sophie, get your mother a chair." He put his hand on Letti's back. "Hold on, *querida*. Kevin's got you. We'll have you sitting down in no time." He looked from Letti to Kevin, and Kevin could have sworn there was amusement in Owen's eyes.

Letti blinked and raised her head. "It's okay. I'm all right now."

Owen caught Kevin's eye and shook his head. The crowd parted as Sophie scurried over with a chair. As gently as they could, Kevin and Wade lowered Letti into the chair and Owen unceremoniously pushed her head down to her knees. Rachel and Maggie escorted the Navarros down the line away from the hubbub and Miranda ushered the audience around the bubble of activity.

Letti tried to raise her head but Owen kept his hand on her neck. "No, Letti. Stay down. It always takes you awhile."

"But…but doesn't she need an ambulance? Doesn't she need a doctor?" Kevin protested.

Owen's lips twitched. "Eventually, maybe. But not tonight."

Letti's mother and grandmother hustled over, followed by his parents. Her mother and grandmother looked at her disbelievingly, and her grandmother crossed herself. "*Dios*," she breathed.

"*Dios* is right," her mother said.

"Oh, d-dear," Kevin's mother said. "Is L-Letti all r-right?"

Letti tried to raise her head but Owen kept his hand on her neck. "Give it another minute or two."

"Let me up," she said. "I'm okay."

Owen moved his hand and Letti jackknifed up. She groaned and held her head. "Damn. I'm more tired than I thought I was."

"Letti, are you sure you're all right?" Kevin said. "Shouldn't we get you to a doctor?"

Wade looked at her doubtfully. "Shouldn't we?" he echoed.

Owen leaned over and whispered something to Wade. Wade's eyes widened into saucers. "Really? Ya think?" He looked at Letti again and he and Owen burst out laughing.

"Daddy, what are you laughing at?" Sophie protested. "Mom nearly passed out."

Kevin looked at them in disgust. "This is *not* funny," he snapped.

"Yeah, it is. Congratulations, Daddy." Owen's eyes were full of unholy glee.

"What?" *What did Owen say to him?*

"I congratulated you. Letti spent most of her other two pregnancies with her head between her knees. Never had a light-headed moment otherwise. No reason to think this is any different."

"Pregnant?" Kevin cringed at the squeak in his voice. "Letti could be pregnant?"

Marco's eyes rounded. "Pregnant? Mom wouldn't do *that*."

"The hell she wouldn't," Sophie shot back. "Pregnant, huh. Better her than me."

"Amen to that," Owen murmured.

Letti scowled at Owen. "It's simply not possible. Menopause, remember? You can't get pregnant during menopause."

"Oh, yes you can. My mom was forty-three when I was born," Owen stated.

"K-Kevin was a m-menop-pause baby," Barbara said. "H-happiest surp-prise ever."

"It happens." His father's face wore the slightest of satisfied smirks as he looked at Letti He turned and winked at Kevin.

"But...but I hadn't had a period in forever when we—" She stammered to a halt and her face turned red. She put her hand over her mouth. "Everybody's listening. Everybody's gonna know my business."

Kevin looked around. "As noisy as it is in here, they can't hear a damned thing." He knelt in front of her. "Letti, what do you think? Is it possible?"

Her eyes were wide as she looked at him. "I don't know. I swear I don't know. I didn't think I even could. But..." She shrugged.

Owen put his hand on Kevin's shoulder. "Only one way to find out. But I'd be willing to bet my income for the next quarter she's carrying a little Summerset in there."

Kevin looked at Letti in wonder. *His baby.* She could be carrying his baby.

He couldn't quite wrap his head around it.

He looked around at the circle enclosing them. His parents. Her mother and grandmother. Owen. Wade. Sophie. Marco. All looking at them with hope in their eyes. Even the kids.

This baby will be so loved.

That is, if Owen was right and there really was a baby.

He and Letti looked at one another. He slowly drew her to her feet. "Folks, Letti and I seem to have another errand to run tonight. We'll talk to you all tomorrow."

"Will you at l-least l-let us k-know?" his mother asked.

"We'll text," he said. "Letti, are you ready to go?"

She nodded. They started through the lobby, only to have her grandmother push her walker over to block Letti's path. The old lady's eyes were burning as she looked at her granddaughter. "*Te dije*, Letti. I told you that you would be blessed. *Verdad*?"

Letti's eyes filled with tears. "You did, *Abuela*. I should have had more faith."

They changed out of their costumes and washed the stage makeup from their faces. He whisked her out the back door and into his car. "Feeling any better?"

"Honestly? No."

"Would some fresh air help?"

Letti nodded and he lowered the top. His hands trembled on the steering wheel as he drove to the all-night pharmacy a few blocks from her house. *A baby.* She could be carrying his baby.

He had never hoped so hard for anything in his life.

She wanted to go straight to her house, but he insisted on picking up tacos. "You nearly passed out tonight. You need something in your stomach. Have you been eating properly?"

"Haven't been hungry."

"How have you been feeling?"

She was quiet a minute. "Sad. Lonely. Missing you. Tired all the time. Feeling shitty a lot." She turned to him. "What if I'm not pregnant? What if we're getting our hopes up for nothing?"

"What if we aren't? Letti, you go pee on a stick and take it from there."

He followed her into her darkened house and handed her the drugstore sack. "Go on up. I'll put these in the oven to stay warm and be there in a minute."

He left the tacos in the oven and took the stairs two at a time. The bathroom door was shut and he banged on it. Letti opened it with a scowl on her face. "Some things need to be private," she groused.

"Better get over that. When I marry you and move in here, I'll see a lot more than you on the potty sometimes."

"Marry me?"

He drew himself up to his full height. "Of course. Summersets don't have babies out of wedlock."

"It's not that simple," she protested.

"Yes, it is. Look at the stick, Letti. Are you or aren't you?"

"I'm scared to look. I want it so bad." She wiped a tear from her eye. "It would be everything I've ever dreamed of."

"Hand it here and let me look at it then."

"I'll look." She peeked at the back of the box and looked at the stick. And sucked in her breath in a gasp. "Look. Two pink lines." She stared for a moment before launching herself at him and throwing her arms around his neck, her tears wetting his cheek and the collar of his shirt.

He wrapped his arms around her. "I'll take that as a yes."

Letti nodded. "I'm so happy," she wailed.

He held on tightly and whirled her around in a circle, tears of joy flowing from his eyes as he held the woman he loved. They clung to one another for long moments, sharing the joy and the wonder of this magical moment.

Letti was in his arms and she carried the start of the family he wanted with all his heart. Everything he'd ever wanted was in his arms.

Life didn't get much better than this.

Chapter Eighteen

Letti's felt herself drift up from the loveliest dream she could remember having in a long time. She and Kevin were on the playground at the nearby park. She was sitting on a picnic table bench near the swing set. The sun was shining and the air was warm. Kevin was standing behind one of the swings in his trademark shorts and flip-flops. His hair was tousled by the wind and he was pushing a tiny dark-haired little girl in a swing. *"Higher, Daddy, higher!" He laughed and pushed her a shade higher. The child turned to Letti. "Look, Mommy. Look at me!"*

Letti felt the dream fade. *No, I don't want to wake up*, she railed to her subconscious. *I want to stay here. I want to dream this beautiful dream some more.* Especially since it was never going to come true…

Her eyes snapped open and she blinked. Pink morning light filtered from behind the blinds. She could hear soft breaths near her ear and feel the lightest of puffs stirring her hair. A muscular chest warmed her back and gentle fingers cradled her lower tummy. Confusion swamped her for a minute, then she recalled the events of last night.

Feeling terrible at the theater. Bloody Mary. Kind words from the Navarros. Practically passing out in front of everyone. The positive pregnancy test. Her tears of joy. His tears of joy. Firing off texts. Eating tacos. Falling into bed, too tired to make love even though she wanted to. Going to sleep in Kevin's arms.

On second thought, she could go back to sleep and dream later. Being awake this morning was pretty damned wonderful.

She snuggled in a little closer. They needed to talk. Pregnancy or not, they still faced issues. More than most couples, given the age difference. Last night's giddy joy notwithstanding, their future still wasn't a slam dunk.

Although things were vastly more hopeful than before.

She slipped out of bed, hoping she didn't wake Kevin, and visited the bathroom. But he was awake when she came out, leaning on his elbow and grinning like a fool. "Well, lookee here. Mama's awake." His grin dimmed a bit. "Are you feeling okay this morning?"

"A hell of a lot better than I did last night. Damn, I'm sorry about conking out on you. I wanted to make love. I really did."

His grin faded entirely. "Don't be ridiculous. You were exhausted and nearly passed out. I'm not that big a sex fiend."

"What a shame," she teased. "I love that young sex fiend."

"And I love my sexy Letti." He waggled his eyebrows. "We can always make up last night's deficit, you know." He picked up the covers. "Come back to bed. We can do that right now."

Letti didn't have to be asked twice. She whipped her knit sleep tank over her head and kicked out of the matching tap pants. Kevin hopped up long enough to make a pit stop in the bathroom, leaving his boxers on the floor on the way back. The sheets were still warm when they met in the middle of the bed. Kevin captured her lips in a long, lingering kiss before abruptly pulling away. "Should we be doing this? Will it hurt the baby?"

She locked her arms around his neck. "It won't hurt the baby. If anything, all the nice pheromones will make the baby that much happier."

"Anything to make the baby happy."

He resumed their passionate kiss. Letti breathed in the scent of Kevin's body close to her. It felt like heaven to be back in his arms. She had missed him so much. His kiss. His touch. His smile. His snarky sense of humor. The way their bodies fit together. The way their minds and hearts fit together. She had missed him to the depths of her soul.

Kevin was "it" for her and always would be.

They shared long, tender, passionate kisses, touching and caressing and nibbling. Every nerve ending in Letti's body was coming alive under his tender touch. Her body was on fire for this man. Together like this, nothing else mattered but him and her. Not his age. Not hers. Nothing mattered in this moment but Kevin and Letti and what they shared together.

They continued their exploration, their kisses growing more passionate before Kevin began a leisurely exploration of her body.

He nuzzled her neck as she nibbled his ear. His lips continued their sexy foray downward, kissing and touching and nibbling her breast and finally to her engorged nipple, which stung with tingles of the not altogether pleasant variety. "Ow," she said, gently nudging his lips away.

"Huh? I thought you liked that."

"Normally I do, but right now it hurts. Pregnancy boobs."

"Sorry. You didn't know it was gonna hurt?"

"Nobody's been nibbling on them lately."

He pulled back the sheet and stared at her breasts. "They're bigger. Prettier." He touched the tip of one with his finger. "So yummy."

She ran her hand down his face. "I've probably had other pregnancy signs as well. I was so convinced I was in menopause I missed them." She cradled his face between her palms. "Shall we pick up where we left off?"

"Am I gonna hurt you anyplace else?"

"No, most of it's going to feel a lot better." She grinned mischievously. "Let's find out."

"Happy to oblige."

They kissed again, touching and stroking, their touches growing more intimate. Kevin caressed her lower stomach. "I can't believe my baby's in there. How big is she?"

Letti covered his hand with hers. "I have no idea. We had unprotected sex for six weeks. I could have gotten pregnant any time in there."

"Will the doctor be able to tell?"

"Probably. We can worry about it later."

"We have more pressing matters to attend to. Like how many times can a pregnant lady come on Sunday morning."

It would be interesting to find out.

Kevin's lips drifted lower and motioned for her to open her legs. He pushed her lower lips apart and stared for a moment. "You look different down here. Fuller, somehow." He raised his head. "Is it gonna hurt down here too?"

"I hope not, as turned on as I am right now."

He slid down and ran his tongue down the slit. "Is that okay?"

"Fucking wonderful. Feels damn good," she moaned when he parted her and found her sensitive nub. He knew exactly how she liked to be touched and within minutes had her clutching the sheets and moaning his name as she toppled over the edge. She came and came and came, her breath coming in gasps as she sank into the sheets.

"Pregnancy orgasms. Gotta love 'em."

"Does it stay like that the entire time?"

"Pretty much, if memory serves."

"We're gonna take advantage of it, then. Lots." His grin was infectious as he lowered his head for round two.

Letti had two more orgasms before Kevin slid up and eased between her legs. She wrapped her arms around him as he slid into her, his body warm and strong over hers. He was still for a minute, both of them savoring the pleasure of their reunion, before he began moving above her, slowly at first, and then with more passion.

Higher and faster they rose together, at one in heart and spirit as well as body. Letti cried out as she felt herself start to climax. Kevin thrust twice more and then he too toppled over the edge, calling her name as his seed spilled into her body, powerful jets pumping into her as she pulsed around him.

They held one another for long moments, savoring the pulsing aftershocks. Then Kevin withdrew and pulled her close, spooning with her back to his chest as he cradled her tummy. "We're going to spend a lot of the next few months like this. Me holding you and our little one."

"Kevin, we need to talk. We still have issues we need to discuss, and we really need to be dressed and sitting on a sofa when we do."

Letti started to pull away but Kevin's arms tightened around her. "Yes, we do need to talk. But this is where we're doing it. In one another's arms, where we'll remember what's really important and won't get distracted by a lot of stuff that's irrelevant."

He rubbed a little circle on her stomach. "While I hold you and our baby. Problems don't seem so insurmountable when we're like this." Letti started to argue but Kevin placed a kiss on the back of her neck. "Now what was it you wanted to say to me?" he asked.

"We're still fifteen years apart."

"So?" She felt his fingers tighten on her stomach. "We've been fifteen years apart since you seduced me in that Holiday Inn hotel room. We were fifteen years apart when we fell in love. We were fifteen years apart when we made a baby together. It doesn't matter. It never has."

"What's that old saying? It doesn't matter until it does. I'll be old long before you will. You'll only be sixty-five when I'm turning eighty. I'll be too old to go on that round-the-world trip that comes with your Medicare card."

"We won't wait until I'm sixty-five to start living. We won't wait for me to get a Medicare card. We'll take our round-the-world trip when you get your Medicare card. We'll go and do as much as we can while we can. That work for you?"

"I guess. What about children?"

"I thought we had that covered," Kevin said as he gave her stomach a gentle rub.

"We have one covered. We managed to conceive one menopause baby. I doubt we will conceive a second."

"There's adoption. There's surrogacy. If we want more we can figure it out when the time comes. Letti, I was ready to beg you to come back *before* we knew about the baby. She's icing on the cake. I love you, woman. I want you beside me for the rest of our lives, raising babies and acting at the Durango, and teaching, and practicing law, and doing whatever else we do."

"You'll be studying with a baby on your shoulder, and I'll be looking at her through my bifocals," she teased. "Are you sure I'm not too old for you?"

"You're not too old for one damned thing. It's all yours for the taking. If anything, Letti, you're now starting the second act of your life."

Epilogue

Josh leaned against the back wall and watched the second act of the Durango Street Theatre's production of *South Pacific*. This performance and one more, and they would put the production to bed and start gearing up for *Peter Pan,* which would run during the holiday season. The *Peter Pan* cast had already been chosen and rehearsals begun, and according to guest director Damon Ortega, one of Letti Aldrete's colleagues from the local community college, the show was taking shape nicely. Letti had been his first choice to direct, but pregnancy at forty was kicking her ass, and her soon-to-be husband persuaded her that her health and that of the baby were more important than a production at the theater. Kevin was right, of course. But it brought home to Josh the kind of sacrifices Letti and Kevin would be making for the next twenty years or so. He couldn't imagine why Letti, who'd already raised one family, was so happy to take on the responsibility once again. But she was thrilled about the baby and more than willing to make the sacrifice. That was all that mattered.

That kind of sacrifice was the last thing he wanted in his life.

Not that it would ever be an issue for him. He was gay. He was unattached and planned to stay that way. A family was not on his horizon in any way, shape, or form.

Thank god.

He turned his attention back to the production. Kevin's Joseph Cable had blown off Liat, and Letti had delivered Bloody Mary's "You stingy bastard" line. It was time for Cameron Heiser's Emile de Becque to sing "This Nearly was Mine," the heart-wrenching lament of lost love. It was also Cameron's best scene in the entire play, his character's heartbreak over the loss of Nellie prompting him to put his life on the line in the allied cause.

Josh stared up at the stage, his eyes taking in every one of Cameron's gestures, his ears hearing every note. He was glad the theater was dark. Otherwise, the lust and longing he kept hidden from the world would be evident for everyone at the theater to see.

He had the hots for Cameron Heiser, big time. He'd gotten bitten by the Cameron bug ever since he'd first laid eyes on the board chairman three and a half years ago. The man topped six feet by a couple of inches and had the kind of lean and rangy body that Josh had always admired in a man. The sport coats and dress pants he usually wore as president of Heiser Steel emphasized the breadth of his shoulders, but did little otherwise to showcase his fantastic body. But he'd come to the theater a few times in his welding clothes, and in a tight tee and work jeans, every delectable inch of his delicious body could be seen and appreciated. Even steel-toed boots were sexy on him. His face was too long and thin, his nose was too big and his cheekbones too prominent for him to be out-and-out handsome, but his blue eyes sparkled and his face radiated intelligence. His wide mouth was made for kissing. The biggest plus, he was gay, although he wasn't especially open about it.

Cameron Heiser was one fine piece of man candy. He could be more, if Josh finally got up the courage to make his move.

The song ended and the stage went dark for a scene change. A few more scenes and the show would be over. The cast would shake hands with the audience and take off their costumes. And most of them would head down the street to Thirties, the old deco bar that had become the unofficial hangout for the Durango's twenty-something crowd. Cameron too, most nights, even though he was considerably older than the rest of the Thirties crowd. Which was why Josh had never acted on the intense attraction he felt. He'd only been twenty-five when he first landed the job at the Durango, after his meteoric rise in the San Antonio theater world. Cameron, chairman of the board and Josh's boss, already had thirty-five in his rear-view mirror and possessed a worldliness and sophistication Josh could only aspire to someday.

But Josh had learned a lot in the last few years, and his confidence had grown in leaps and bounds. He wasn't a gauche kid anymore. There was no reason he and Cameron couldn't get together.

Lately, he'd seen from a front row seat that an age gap didn't have to be a big deal. Wade and Owen were fifteen years apart and it didn't seem to affect their relationship one bit. Letti's soon-to-be husband was twenty-five to her forty. It had been an issue for them at first, but now they were like any other couple looking forward to marriage and parenthood.

If it didn't matter for those two couples, it shouldn't matter for him and Cameron.

Not that he was looking for anything permanent. But he was tired of lusting after Cameron from afar. He wanted to get up close and personal. He wanted to go out on a date and talk about something other than theater business. He wanted to see if the attraction was mutual. If it was, he wanted to act on it.

He'd make his move tonight. It would be subtle, but gay men in San Antonio were used to subtle. If Cameron turned him down, then at least he tried.

If Cameron took him up on it, they'd see what happened.

Josh was thinking about the evening to come when his phone vibrated in his pocket. He started to ignore the buzz and let the call go to voice mail. But something, he wasn't sure what, prompted him to look at the phone and he frowned. Bubbe's name and phone number glowed on the screen. Definitely not the norm for his grandmother. Clara Goldstein had turned ninety-one a month ago, and was never up past eight at night. Something was up.

He jogged to the lobby and tried to catch the call but was too late. He hit the "call" button and got her on the third try. "Are you all right, Bubbe?"

"I'm fine, Joshie. Fine."

But she didn't sound fine. Her Austrian accent was thicker than usual, a sure-fire tell that she was stressed. Plus, she sounded weary. "What is it, Bubbe?" he demanded.

She hesitated for a moment. "It's Miriam, Joshie. She's here. She and the kids drove in a few minutes ago. She needs to talk to you."

Miriam. The older sister he loved so much who he hadn't seen in way too long. "She drove here all the way from Bumfuck, Mississippi with two little kids in the car? Did she say why she came?"

"Just…just come, Joshie." Bubbe's voice broke. "She'll explain it when you get here." His grandmother disconnected.

Something was definitely wrong. If he hurried, he could make it to Bubbe's in fifteen minutes.

He shot off a text to Rachel to cover him greeting the audience. He took one more peek in the theater. Cameron's Emile de Becque was hunkered down behind a rock spying on the Japanese. Josh looked at Cameron wistfully.

So much for seducing his favorite fantasy.

Tonight family came first.

ABOUT THE AUTHOR

The author of over forty romance novels, Emily Mims combined her writing career with a career in public education until leaving the classroom to write full time. The mother of two sons, she and her husband split their time between central Texas, eastern Tennessee, and overseas visiting their kids and grandchildren. For relaxation Emily plays the piano, organ, dulcimer, and ukulele for two different performing groups, and even sings a little. She says, "I love to write romances because I believe in them. Romance happened to me and it can happen to any woman—if she'll just let it."

Connect with Emily:
facebook.com/emily.mims.756
twitter.com/emilymimsauthor
instagram.com/mims_emily
website: emilymims.com

www.BOROUGHSPUBLISHINGGROUP.com

If you enjoyed this book, please write a review. Our authors appreciate the feedback, and it helps future readers find books they love. We welcome your comments and invite you to send them to info@boroughspublishinggroup.com. Follow us on Facebook, Twitter and Instagram, and be sure to sign up for our newsletter for surprises and new releases from your favorite authors.

Are you an aspiring writer? Check out www.boroughspublishinggroup.com/submit and see if we can help you make your dreams come true.

www.ingramcontent.com/pod-product-compliance
Lightning Source LLC
Chambersburg PA
CBHW020128180626
46810CB00004B/1447